To David,

Here you go, David —
your own copy. I hope
you enjoy it!
Uncle John

# The Green Eyed Girl

## J. W. Chew

authorHOUSE®

*AuthorHouse™ UK*
*1663 Liberty Drive*
*Bloomington, IN 47403 USA*
*www.authorhouse.co.uk*
*Phone: 0800.197.4150*

*Published by AuthorHouse 12/16/2014*

*ISBN: 978-1-4969-9919-1 (sc)*
*ISBN: 978-1-4969-9920-7 (hc)*
*ISBN: 978-1-4969-9921-4 (e)*

# *Prologue*

As the girl walked into the village all heads turned. It was not her beauty that attracted attention, it was her eyes. Eyes the deep, impossible green of fine emeralds. Eyes that pierced the soul, looking not at you but through you. Unfathomable eyes. Expressionless eyes. Eyes that would haunt your dreams.

She was tall, slender and strong. Her hair, raven black, hung tangled and unkempt to her waist. Her clothing was bizarre at best. Heavy, brown leather riding breaches, much mended and patched, were coupled with a man's silk shirt in blue, once fine but now faded and torn. Both were two large for her by far. On her feet were boots, yet not a pair. The apparel could have been chosen entirely at random.

By the time she reached the middle of the village the people were already gathering. The farrier, his mind wrenched from the red hot iron of the horseshoe on his anvil, left his hammer hanging in mid air between one stroke and the next. The voices of the children faded to silence. The gossip of the village women died on their lips. All minds turned to her. Time itself stood still, and stillest of all stood the girl.

As if carved of granite she stood. Set to stone. There was no flicker of eye, no smile, no turn of head or glance. Nothing but the soft wafting of raven hair in the spring breeze. All waited. All watched. All listened.

Then she spoke. "I seek to learn the ways of men."

It was a deep voice and oddly flat. A voice with no rise, no fall, no intonation or expression. The accent was also strange, words plucked from the mind and then forced from an unsure mouth.

Clang! An ache in the farrier's shoulder reminded him of his raised hammer and he dropped it to the anvil. The girl's head turned to the new sound. A sudden, sharp turn, followed once more by stillness.

She looked into his eyes and repeated, "I seek to learn the ways of men."

The might of the glance, the sheer power and intensity of her eyes, drove him back first one step and then another. His gaze dropped to her feet. "I don't know what you mean, miss," he stammered.

A pause. A consideration. "I have come far," she said. "My place is different to this place. I know nothing of the ways of men. The manners of men. The actions and thoughts of men. I desire to learn so that I may live among mankind. I seek to learn the ways of men."

"Who ...?" It was one of the village women, but her question died on her lips as she, like the farrier, found herself assaulted by emerald eyes. She stopped, regathered her thoughts, and started again. "Who are you, my dear?"

"You ask my name?"

"Well ... yes ... maybe."

"I have a name," the girl said, "yet it is a name for another place and other company. I have no name for this place. I need such a name. Name me."

The woman looked nervously to her companions. There were unsure gestures. Shrugs. The murmur of quiet words. "You want us to <u>give</u> you a name, my dear?"

"Yes," the girl replied. "A name that is right for this place. A name I can be known by here."

More unsure glances and gestures. More whispers caught on the breeze, then another woman spoke. "I had a daughter," she said, "who would have been near your age, miss, had she not been taken from us by a fever some years ago. Her name was Lyssa."

"Lyssa will serve," said the girl. "I am Lyssa. I have something I believe is prized." At her waist was a small belt pouch. Into this she plunged her hand and withdrew it. She stretched out her arm and opened her fingers to reveal the glitter of gold. "I understand this is considered of worth by men."

There was a gasp. A small village of subsistence farmers rarely saw silver, let alone gold. One of the women reacted in alarm. "For God's sake, girl, put that away!"

A pause. A quizzical look. "It is not prized?"

"It is prized!" snapped the woman. "Prized too much for you to openly carry such wealth in these troubled times!"

"Wealth?"

"The coins, girl! Money! Gold!"

"Put them away, lass," the farrier murmured. "There are those who would hurt you to take the coins from you."

The girl looked down at her hand. "Gold," she said. "A yellow metal, heavy and soft. No use for tool or weapon, and yet men would seek my harm to take these ... coins?"

"They would." The farrier stepped forward and gently wrapped her fingers back around the gold. "Put them away, lass, and don't bring them out again until you need them."

She returned the coins to her belt pouch and looked up into the farrier's face. "Teach me of gold."

The farrier chucked. "I know little of gold, miss, I've not held gold coin in my hand for many a year. It is money, a means of exchange. It is prized because it can be bartered for other things of value. For food, shelter, firewood, iron, wine and so on. Truth be told, lass, that gold in your pouch could buy this village whole."

There was no expression in her face. No sign or either understanding or puzzlement. "I could exchange this gold for food and shelter?"

"Certainly," the farrier replied. "One coin alone would feed, clothe and home you for many a month if that was your desire."

She considered. "That is my desire."

The farrier frowned. "Why? This is a village. Simple people living their lives in the fields and workshops. We have nothing here. Few pleasures besides ale and song. Two dozen men, women and children living in houses of wattle and daub. What is there here for you?"

"I seek to learn the ways of men," she replied. "Will you teach me? Can I exchange the gold so prized for the knowledge I need?"

The farrier looked at the other villagers. There were wordless glances, shrugged shoulders, but then nods. He turned back to the girl. "In God's name, miss, who <u>are</u> you?"

"You know who I am," she replied. "I'm Lyssa."

# Chapter One

Twenty-two years later.

Lyssa sat on a rock and pulled her cloak tight around her. It was not the bitter mountain wind that chilled her, despite it being mid winter beneath a snow-filled sky. There was an ice in her veins that had nothing to do with the weather. An ice in her heart and soul.

She looked up the mountain slope above her. Crumpled over the bare rock and moss was a shape, the vast shape of a dragon. Its body was shattered. Its bones broken. Its skull smashed. Blood stained the stone of the mountain side, a patch of rust brown on the grey. Three deep, ragged claw gashes in the moss spoke of one last, anguished kick. A brilliant green eye glared, still open though blind in death. Lyssa took a deep breath, closed her eyes against the sight, and sighed.

She didn't know how she felt. There was a desolation, almost as desolate as the bare, barren rocks around her. A crushing sense of waste. Deep, sickening sorrow that knotted her stomach. And guilt, of course. Overwhelming all else was guilt.

She stood and turned down slope. Below her was a narrow road, perhaps just a track, winding through the mountains. There stood her horse, tethered to a coarse bush behind which it was trying to shelter from the harsh wind. He looked less than delighted to be there, but at least he would soon have company. Further along the road two riders approached, unknown but not unexpected. She watched them dismount and tether their beasts, then they began to climb towards her.

One, most certainly, was a fine gentleman. He was tall, dark of hair and firm of glance, perhaps in his mid thirties. His riding breeches and shirt were matched in dark, green velvet. On his head a hat, also velvet but brown, sported a long plume. He pulled around him a great cloak, edged with fur and fastened with a glittering brooch of gold and garnet. His boots gleamed with fresh polish and, as he approached, she saw the glitter of jewel on finger.

The other was older and less richly dressed. His attire was good and functional, but wool. His shirt and breeches were both brown, but of different shade. His boots scuffed, the sign of hard use. His riding cloak showed signs of repair and was fastened with a pin rather than a brooch. He wore no hat, perhaps needing none due to shaggy, greying hair and heavy beard.

They approached and stopped, but while the well dressed gentleman's eyes turned to Lyssa, his companion looked not at her but past her to the dead dragon beyond.

"Good morning miss," the gentleman said. "Allow me to introduce myself. I am Lord Norras Farron, aid to Duke Telchar Bliss. With me is Mr Aldon Torm, the renowned expert on all matters dragon."

Lyssa murmured a greeting. The man Torm made an indistinct noise she assumed to be a reply, but in truth his mind was already elsewhere.

Farron extracted a small book of writing slates from within his cloak. To this he referred. "You are ... Miss Lyssa Gort?"

"Yes."

He nodded. "I understand you were travelling the road below accompanied by a local copper miner when you saw the fallen dragon. You instructed your companion to inform us while you remained here."

"Not quite," Lyssa murmured. "The miner recalled both your Lordship and Mr Torm were visiting a nearby village. It was he who felt you should be informed."

"Good man." Farron made a note on his slate. "He was right to do so. Did you see any sign of life in the beast when you first arrived?"

"No." Lyssa's voice was flat. "She was already dead."

"She …?" Farron frowned and looked up. "... Ah yes. Well spotted, young lady. A cow dragon indeed."

Lyssa fractionally straightened. Yes, dragons were often referred to as cows and bulls to indicate gender but she had always felt uncomfortable with the terms. They seemed … unfitting.

Farron turned to Torm. "So what do you see, my friend?"

Torm frowned. "Things I don't understand," he murmured. "Let me look closer, my Lord."

"Of course."

Torm left them and approached the corpse. He circled and examined. He ran his fingers through his hair and frowned.

Farron chuckled. "He's a good man," he assured Lyssa. "A bit odd, I admit, but a good man. We don't often find dragons like this and when we do we like to work out what happened. None do that like Torm. He'll ponder and probe, scratch his head and frown, but in the end he'll get there."

"I'm glad to hear it," Lyssa replied, though she already knew the truth.

For ten further minutes Torm circled and examined, then he called. "The immediate cause of death is easy enough. She has suffered multiple, massive injuries. Her skull, both forelegs, both shoulders and her forward chest all shattered by impact. There's no sign on violence on her, either of human or dragon origin, so she died when she hit the ground."

Farron nodded. "She got her landing wrong?"

Lyssa opened her mouth to object, but Torm saved her the effort.

"No, my Lord. That cannot be, and on two counts." He continued his examination as he spoke. His frown got, if possible, deeper. "Firstly her head lies down the slope towards the road. No dragon would try to land down this slope so she wasn't tying to land at all. Secondly when a dragon lands she drops her hips, lifts her shoulders and cups her wings forward to bleed off her speed. At the moment of landing her wings are stalled, her speed is low and she drops onto her rear legs first." He illustrated with his hand. "Her forefeet touch down second, yet this dragon's injuries are to the <u>front</u> of her body."

Farron joined Torm in a frown. "So she hit the ground head first?"

"That's how I read it," Torm replied, "very steep and very fast. Look, my Lord, see how her forelegs and shoulders are smashed. She tried to stretch them out to save herself as she struck, but nothing could save her."

Unseen by the two men Lyssa nodded. Torm's reading of the signs matched her own, as far as it went, yet would he also see the rest? She offered a prompt. "Why?"

Torm turned back towards her. "That is an excellent ques ..." For the first time he properly looked at her and his voice failed mid word. His eyes widened. His jaw dropped.

4

And Farron laughed. "May the Gods preserve us Torm! I swear I've never before seen <u>you</u> stunned to silence by a pretty face. There is hope for you yet, my friend. Perhaps you should invite the young lady to dinner!"

Torm regained his composure and, with apparent difficulty, pulled his gaze from Lyssa. "I suspect, my Lord," he almost whispered, "that I am not her type, yet her question cuts to the heart of the matter. Look at the dragon, my Lord. Forget the obvious injuries. True, they killed her, but they are a symptom of the real problem, not its cause. Look at <u>her</u>."

Farron's mirth faded, replaced with puzzlement. He turned, and stepped, and looked. "I'm not sure what you drive at, my friend," he said. "Your eyes are better trained to this task than mine, yet ..." his head tilted slightly "... she does appear somewhat underfed."

"Somewhat underfed?" For Lyssa the understatement made continued silence impossible. "Her ribs stand out like mountain ridges! Her legs, her neck, her shoulders, all wasted. Her flight muscles practically non-existent. She wasn't 'somewhat underfed' my Lord, she was starving to the verge of death. The surprise is not that she fell out of the sky. The surprise, indeed the miracle, is that she managed to get off the ground in the first place."

Farron turned and looked at Lyssa with increased curiosity. "You appear remarkably confident in your observations, young lady," he observed. "Torm, do you also read the matter as Miss Gort has read it?"

"I could not have put the point better myself, my Lord," Torm replied. "This dragon was doomed long before her last flight. Starved to the point of no return. Today she flew in desperation, for nothing but desperation would have forced her into the air in this condition. She sought something, <u>anything</u>, that she could eat. Anything that could delay her end by a few more hours or days, yet her wings failed her. They collapsed and she fell. Yes, her body was shattered by impact but in truth it was starvation that killed her. Her life ended in despair, terror and shattering pain, yet perhaps even that was a mercy at the end."

Lyssa nodded. That was the truth she had, herself, seen. Yet it was still not the whole truth. As before she prompted. "Why?"

"Because of us," Torm answered grimly.

Farron's eyes shifted from Torm to Lyssa and back to Torm. "Because of us? She starved because of us? 'Us' personally, or 'us' humanity in general?"

"'Us' humanity in general," Torm replied, "or, to be precise, the humanity that lives in these mountains. Mountain creatures are shy and timid at best. Humans fill the mountains with bustle, the noise of voice and hammer and chisel, and everything that can flee does. The mountains become barren and empty." He glanced at Farron and then looked around at the mountains that surrounded them. "When did you last see a mountain goat in these parts, my Lord?"

"A goat? Why, I last saw one ... well ... I think it was ..." he lapsed into silence.

"As long ago as that, my Lord?" asked Lyssa, an edge of sarcasm in her voice. "I can answer the question for myself, because I made mental note of the sight. For me it was a little over nine weeks ago."

"Yet go back ten years," Torm observed, "and you could have stood where we now stand, scanned the mountains with your naked eye, and seen a half dozen. Dragons can't live on water and air alone, my Lord. We killed this dragon as surely as if we had taken axes and hacked off her head. The disturbing thing is this dragon's age. I would guess she is some six or seven hundred years ..." He looked to Lyssa for confirmation.

"About that."

"... and a dragon might expect to live between a thousand and fifteen hundred. This dragon was not young and weak, or old and weak. When starvation kills the young and old we have a problem. When it kills those who should be strong we have a disaster. Doubly so as the dragons are fighting back."

"Fighting back?" Farron frowned.

"Dragon attacks, my Lord."

Farron was dismissive. "Nonsense, Torm! I accept dragons attack the occasional wagon train, but that's not 'fighting back'. They attack so they can eat the horses!"

"And mines?" Torm asked. "Why do dragons attack mines, my Lord? There are no horses there. What about the mining villages? The people cut bolt-holes and flee to them for safety when dragons strike, so thankfully the number of deaths are low, but when the dragons are gone and they return to their homes they find them utterly destroyed. Why would a dragon trouble itself to flame and smash houses and workshops? Not for food, there is none. These aren't dragons <u>hunting</u>. These are dragons <u>fighting</u>. These are dragons actively seeking to drive humans out of the mountains. We are <u>at war</u>, my Lord. We just haven't woken up to it yet."

Farron almost laughed. "If we are at war, my friend, then it is a war the dragons cannot possibly win. Yes, they kill a few people, which is deeply unfortunate. I wish they did not, but ultimately more people die in accidents than dragon attacks. They destroy a few buildings, which we re-build within months. Dragons are an inconvenience rather than a genuine threat. They have no way to hurt us."

"Unless they <u>find</u> a way," Torm observed.

"They won't," Farron replied. "And even if they did, we would find a way to counter their new threat. Remember how dragons used to attack our mountain cities? We devised defences that could drive the dragons back, leaving many of them dead. There hasn't been a

7

dragon attack on a mountain city for over two decades now. They <u>know</u> they can't win!"

Torm ran his fingers through his hair. "Maybe you're right, my Lord. Time will tell, yet I still believe we underestimate dragons at our greatest peril. Particularly when our activity in the mountains is starving hundreds of them into desperation. We might just push them into doing something we <u>deeply</u> regret."

Farron considered for twenty seconds at least. "I hear your words, my friend," he said, "and I respect them, yet I cannot see the threat you fear."

"Can you see the injustice of dragons starving to death because of human activity in the mountains," Lyssa asked.

Farron chuckled. "It seems Torm is not unique in his love of dragonkind." Then the smile faded. "Yet I accept you ask a fair question. Yes, I can see it as an injustice but what is the solution? If the people of these mountains were forced to leave, so the goats would return, that would be an injustice for <u>them</u>. The livelihoods of good men and women depend on the copper and tin. They do not sink mines out of malice to dragonkind, they sink them to put a roof over their children's heads. To feed and clothe them. I am sorry, <u>genuinely</u> sorry, that this dragon suffered as she did. She deserved better, and I wish her well in whatever afterlife dragons believe in. My loyalty, however, is always for my own kind." He consciously set the matter aside. "Now, I don't know about anyone else but I believe our work here is done. I plan to find the nearest inn and buy a good meal and good wine. I would be delighted if you two would join me."

Lyssa took a deep breath and slowly expelled it. "Thank you, my Lord, but I think I shall stay here."

"Why?" Farron asked.

"Just to keep her company a while."

"I would advise against it," Farron said. "The mountains are not a safe place for a woman alone."

"I hear your advise, my Lord."

"Very well," Farron conceded, "it's your decision. Torm? Will you join me for food and wine?"

Torm glanced at Lyssa then back to Farron. "Ride on ahead, my Lord. I will catch up with you. I would like to have a few private words with this young lady."

"Very well." Farron made his way down the slope to the road.

Torm watched him a while, to ensure he was well out of earshot, then turned to Lyssa. "What is your name, young lady?"

"Lyssa Gort."

Torm smiled, the smile of a knowing conspirator. "No, young lady, your <u>real</u> name." He glanced pointedly at the dead dragon then reached to Lyssa. Cupping a hand under her chin he raised her eyes to meet his. "Earlier I was stunned to silence, but not by your beauty. I was stunned by your <u>eyes</u>. I know what they mean. All else changes but the colour of your eyes remains the same, doesn't it ..." he leant forwards and whispered "... <u>dragon</u>?"

She tensed for a moment, considering denial. The look in his eyes convinced her there was little point. "I have often wondered if they would betray me."

Torm dropped his hand from her chin. "Then be reassured, young lady, there are few men indeed who have read the accounts I have read. Fewer still who would believe them. Your secret is safe with me."

She nodded. "Then for that I thank you. I also thank you for your words and your understanding. You looked, and you saw, and you spoke the truth."

Torm looked back to the dead dragon. "Did you know her?"

"I should," Lyssa replied. "She laid the egg from which I hatched."

"Oh, sweet God! Your mother?" For a second time there was shock in his eyes. "I'm so sorry! I had no idea this tragedy was personal for you."

"How could you know?" Lyssa whispered. "For twenty-two years I have lived among humans, learning their ways and customs. So many times I have travelled these roads and paths, always looking skyward and wondering if I would see my mother flying above. The last time I saw her was eight or nine months ago and I thought she didn't look well, yet I only saw her from distance and I convinced myself I'd seen wrong. I should have acted. I should have done something then, but I didn't." Tears suddenly flooded into her eyes. "I let her down. I failed her."

"No!" Torm was adamant. "This is <u>not your fault!</u>"

"Ah, but it is," Lyssa murmured. "Your friend the lord Farron understands. Remember his words? He said 'my loyalty is always for my own kind'. That truth I had forgotten. The time has come for me to remember I am a dragon, and where my loyalty lies."

"What will you do?"

"You said we were at war, humankind and dragonkind," Lyssa replied. "Yet lord Farron couldn't see it. I must <u>make</u> him see it. I must make that war real for him, and for the whole of humanity."

"Dear God. How?"

"Hell knows!"

Torm thought a moment before stepping to Lyssa and placing a hand on her shoulder. "You realise, young lady, that I cannot wish you success in 'making this war real' for us?"

"I would not expect you to," she replied. "You are a noble and honourable man, but you are a <u>man</u>. Your loyalty is to your own kind. Now, if I may, I would spend some time alone with my mother. Besides, lord Farron will be expecting you. Take care, and I wish you well."

"As I wish you well also. Farewell." He turned and started to climb down the slope to his tethered horse.

He had barely got twenty feet before she turned and called. "Oh, Torm. One more thing." He looked back at her. "My real name. Khaajd."

He smiled. "Thank you Khaajd." Once more he turned for his horse.

She watched him descend. She watched him mount. She watched him ride out of sight, then she watched the empty road for at least ten more minutes.

Finally she turned and climbed to the dragon above. A human cannot hug a dragon, the difference in size is just too vast. All a human can do is weep. She wept.

# Chapter Two

---

Kaslam was a small market town nestled on the very edge of the mountains. From here a road wound deep into the mountain range itself, climbing steadily until it reached the great 'high mountain' city of Tekmir.

The journey from Kaslam to Tekmir was not one to be taken lightly, or to be attempted alone. The danger was not dragons, even though Lyssa might wish it was, but footpads, bandits and other criminal lowlifes who preyed on the lone traveller. For short trips, where she could travel by day and spend each night in an inn, she put her faith in a fast horse, keen eyes and a sharp dagger at her belt. Yet the road to Tekmir was another matter, nine days of travel and the need to camp at night by the roadside.

For this reason there were two wagon trains that shuttled back and forth, each guarded by a dozen armed men. Travelling with the wagon train were two 'beast wagons' stocked with horse oats and a temporary corral formed of great, canvas wind breaks to shelter horses and ponies from the bitter, winter wind. All were free to join the train, enjoying the protection of the guard and feeding their beasts from the beast wagons, on payment of a fee. The fee was three silver crowns per wagon, or two per person or beast.

The first grey light of pre-dawn shimmered in the east when Lyssa rode into the market square to join the train, a well-loaded pony trudging along behind her riding horse. Already four extra wagons and six horseback riders had gathered. A small, folding table stood in the corner of the square, illuminated by a wind-proof lantern. Behind it, on a stool, sat an armoured man. A rugged looking man with greying hair at his temples. Lyssa made her way to him and he looked up at her.

"You for the train to Tekmir, miss?"

"I am."

"I am Captain Gast. I will be commanding the guard on this trip," he said, then peered. "One person, one riding horse and one pack beast?"

"Correct."

"Six silver if you please, miss," Gast informed her. "I will also need your signature and the name of someone to contact should misfortune befall you."

Lyssa laughed. "Is misfortune likely to befall me, Captain?"

"Not if I or any of my men have a say say in the matter," he replied gruffly, "but should it happen we will try to inform next of kin."

"I fear I am alone in the world," Lyssa said, suddenly softer. "Yet if I am permitted to name someone who is not a relative, there is a man who might care if lived or died. A man called Aldon Torm."

"The dragon man?"

"That's him," Lyssa confirmed. "Unfortunately I don't know where he could be contacted."

"That is not a problem," Gast replied, writing in a small book on the table in front of him. "He's well enough known to be found, if need arises. And you, yourself, are ...?"

"Lyssa Gort."

Again he wrote, and then signalled one of his soldiers forward. "Hold the lady's reign, Dennet, so she can dismount."

A youthful warrior with a broad grin stepped forward to hold Lyssa's reign as she slipped from the saddle. She took six silver coins from her belt pouch and placed them on the table in front of Gast. He put them in a cash box and turned the book to her, offering a pen.

"If you could put your mark there, miss." He indicated the place and she signed. "Thank you. There are few rules on the train, save that we are governed by the local laws wherever we may happen to be. Your beasts may be fed from the beast wagons, but your own food is your concern. Have you made adequate provision?"

"Yes. My pack pony is well stocked."

"Good," he said. "We have a provisioner travelling with us so you might be able to buy extra if you need, but be warned. His prices seem to rise suddenly when he knows his customers have no other option."

"The man has a keen sense of business."

"So he tells me," Gast muttered. "I call him a bloody shark. Now a piece of advise, miss. If we are attacked by brigands or bandits <u>do not flee</u>. My men cannot protect a scattered group."

Lyssa nodded. "And if we are attacked by dragons?"

He gave her a sharp look. "We'll have no trouble with dragons, miss," he growled.

She looked at him for a dozen seconds. "Good," she said. "Where do I go?"

Gast nodded in the direction of the other mounted travellers. "If you'll wait with the other riders, miss," he said. "Any who wish to join us must do so by sunrise. We will leave shortly after that."

Lyssa re-mounted.

The first three days of the journey were relatively easy, climbing gently into the foothills of the mountains. During the day they travelled, with short breaks mid morning and afternoon, and a longer one around noon for a main meal. At night the ponies and horses were corralled with food, water and the wind-breaks for shelter while the people lit oil stoves, cooked another hearty meal and retired for the night. Lyssa had brought a bedroll, several heavy blankets and a small mountain tent for the journey, but actually negotiated to sleep under the shelter of of one of the wagons for a fee. It was the wagon of the shark-like provisioner as it happened, his keen sense of business appreciating the opportunity for further profit.

As the days passed and the road got higher the air got colder. The horses found themselves trudging through deep, fresh-fallen snow. The wagons left great, dark stripes along the pristine, white road. Before long Lyssa found herself shivering and exchanged her light, "lowland" riding cloak for a vastly heavier and thicker item she had packed on her pack pony. It was a magnificent thing, especially made for her, gleaming brilliant scarlet and golden in the mountain light. She pulled it close around her shoulders as the wind blew.

All passed without incident until the late evening of the sixth day. The sun had set, the late meal had been eaten and darkness enveloped them. They were just about to turn to their beds when a distant, bright flare illuminated the night. Lyssa, sitting by the warmth of an oil stove, instantly tensed. The soldiers of the guard likewise.

"Damnation!" It was one of the soldiers. "Go and get the captain. See if he saw it."

"No need." Gast was already hurrying to join them. "I did. Watch and see if it happens again."

Lyssa got to her feet and joined the men, gazing out into the blackness. A minute passed. Two. Then another flare of light erupted into the night. A flame, obviously a flame, flickered high into the sky from a distant mountain top.

"Hell's blood!" Gast cursed. "That was dragon fire for sure!"

"They're attacking something?" One of the other travellers had joined them, her eyes wide and fearful. The provisioner's daughter.

"No," Gast reassured her. "That's not killing flame. When they fight they use their lungs to blow air into their fire, making it burn blue and hot enough to melt glass. That's signal flame. Less air, cooler but brighter."

"They're signalling?" The girl didn't look reassured. "To whom?"

"No idea," muttered Gast. "To another dragon I guess. We used to see signal flame like that in the mountains near Tekmir, back in the days when they attacked the city. The messages didn't seem sophisticated in any way, just 'now' as a signal to do something pre-arranged. Sure as hell, though, there's a dragon watching who knows what he's supposed to do."

"So what do we do ourselves?" asked Lyssa.

"We get to Tekmir," Gast replied, "and hope the dragons don't choose that moment to attack."

"You think they're planning to strike at the city?"

"I'll lay odds they're planning to attack <u>something</u>, miss," Gast growled. "Dragons don't send up signal flame just to say they're off for a flight through the mountains. It'll either be Tekmir or one of the mining villages."

"Or us?" Lyssa offered another option.

Gast chuckled. "We're too small to warrant the attention of dragons, miss," he assured her. "Besides, if they were going to attack us they wouldn't bother signalling. No need. They wouldn't have to co-ordinate several battle dragons against a wagon train. One would suffice." The light flared once more, then diminished. "Not even a big one at that."

For ten further minutes they watched as the distant flame burned and vanished, burned and vanished. Then the normal darkness of night returned. This, too, they watched for at least a further half hour.

Not many slept that night.

The next morning the mood was subdued. Even with Gast's assurances the travellers were nervous. The open mountains were no place to be when dragons were active. Over breakfast there was no other topic of conversation, and while they rode heads turned and eyes scanned, looking for black specks against a grey, snow-laden sky.

Yet they saw nothing. No black specks. Nothing to fear.

The mid morning break was taken quickly and they headed on, still climbing higher into the mountains. There was no idle talk now, as there had been previous days, just a growing sense of tension. It was almost too quiet, too peaceful, too … right.

They stopped for the mid day break.

"Keep this short, ladies and gentlemen," Gast urged them. "The further we go, the sooner we arrive at Tekmir. Every mile counts."

"Yet we must eat, as must the beasts," observed Lyssa, "and I, for one, need to stretch my legs a little after a morning in the saddle."

"Of course we must eat!" Gast sounded irritated. "And if you must walk, do so, but not far or long. We don't want to have to search for you, and we must be on our way within the half hour."

"Half an hour will be fine," Lyssa assured him.

She grabbed some bread and cold, cooked meats, folding them together into a makeshift sandwich. She wrapped her cloak about her and made her way a little off the road to the north. The road itself was just a smoothed track through a rock strewn landscape, so she had to step barely twenty paces before she could slip behind a boulder and disappear from the caravan's view. She discarded her sandwich, a pretence for the eyes of others, and grasped the edges of her scarlet and gold riding cloak. She turned to face the boulder and spread the cloak wide, a shimmering splash of colour against a barren, grey and snow-white landscape.

The signal of the night before had been answered, and now all she could do was wait.

Not for long, as it happened. Away to the north there was an answering flare of white flame, less obvious in the light of day than it had been in the dark of night. She listened. There was no sound of sudden alarm from the wagon train. No cries or shouts. They hadn't noticed.

Good.

She stepped away from the rock and headed north, away from the road. Straying hardly mattered now. Indeed she needed to put as much distance between herself and the wagon train as she could. It would not be long. Minutes at most. All the time she scanned the northern skyline.

Then she saw what she was looking for. One, two, three black shapes lifted over the line of the distant mountains. Dots at first, tiny in the distance, but rapidly enlarging. Three dragons, three massive battle dragons, bore down on them, flying low and fast with powerful,

19

shallow wing beats. Directly towards her they flew, using her scarlet and yellow cloak as a beacon for their flight. In one minute they were transformed from dots into distinct shapes, in one more they were distant no longer. Great wings cupped the air, bleeding off speed, while they were still a mile out. The air roared and thundered. Lyssa's cloak whipped and fresh snow flashed into an instant blizzard as they passed barely twenty feet above her head. Then came another thunderous roar from behind her, a roar of flame accompanied by searing heat that singed her hair and made her dive for cover.

Pandemonium.

Horses didn't whinny, they screamed. The humans screamed. The ground shook under the impact as dragons landed. She heard Gast's voice barking futile commands, but drowning out all was the fury of dragons. They thundered. They snarled. They bellowed. Blasts of flame tore the snow from the mountainsides to send it, as torrents of melt-water, tumbling over the rocks. Lyssa couldn't see, but she knew.

And then, suddenly, all was quiet. Very, very quiet, except for the occasional crunch of a huge claw against the rock or the faint grind of scale. She waited. Waited as the dragons searched for those yet to kill. Waited as two of the three climbed high to launch themselves back into the air. Waited as their wings hissed and roared, beating the protesting air to gain height. Waited as they circled and climbed and, once more, vanished into the northern mountains. Only then did she move out of cover and head back towards the road.

Where the caravan had been there was now nothing but devastation. Wagons shattered to matchwood and scorched by flame. Horses and humans lying in the wreckage, their bodies twisted and broken. Their eyes, even in death, filled with the terrors of their last moments. She looked around and her heart sank. She had known this was coming. She had known it, and planned it, and steeled herself. Yet, for all that, it was still a sight to tear the soul.

"Dear God," she murmured to no-one. "Oh dear God!"

She turned. Amid the wreckage stood the last dragon, the biggest of the three, plucking dead horses from between the shafts of the smashed wagons and bolting them down. For a moment she watched him, then she called out.

"You really should knock the harness off them first, Bhuul. Tanned leather and metal buckles will play havoc with your digestion."

The dragon turned to her, his green eyes meeting her own. In his mouth was a horse, dwarfed by the size of his own head, with neck hanging limply from one side of his jaw and hindquarters hanging from the other. Almost contemptuously he spat out the morsel. It tumbled, hitting the ground with a heavy, crunching thud. Then came a deep rumble. A shaped rumble. Dragon speech. A sound impossible for the human voice to produce, but which the human ear could understand if trained to the task. "I do not require," the monster growled, "advise on how to eat a horse."

Lyssa shrugged, continuing to speak in the human tongue. "Your choice, Bhuul," she warned, "but don't complain to me if you end up with belly ache. Are they all dead?"

"Of course." His massive neck curved as he lowered his head to the dropped horse. Picking up the carcass he flicked it up into the air and caught it, and again until it was positioned to his liking. It disappeared whole. "Now what?" he asked.

"Now," Lyssa murmured, walking among the dead, "I have to die."

Bhuul 'tongue wrapped', twelve feet of forked tongue snaking from his mouth and wrapping itself around his muzzle, first one way and then the other. The dragon equivalent of a grin or chuckle, a sign of amusement. "That I can arrange," he observed.

She looked up at him. His eyes bored into her from thirty feet up. "Indeed," she murmured, "but after I have died I must remain of use. That is a little more difficult." She continued walking among the dead, searching. Eventually she found what she was looking for or, more specifically, who. The provision's daughter matched her closely in build.

Kneeling beside the corpse she slipped off her scarlet and yellow cloak. Lifting the woman's shoulders she fastened the cloak around her and then arranged it as if worn. "I'm sorry," she murmured to un-hearing ears. "Nothing personal." She stood and strode away some two hundred feet. There she turned. "Now, Bhuul," she called. "Make yourself useful. Singe her for me."

The dragon edged towards the dead woman, lowered his head, and seemed merely to cough. A sharp, savage explosion of pale, blue flame erupted from his jaw, striking the body on the ground and shooting sideways. Even from two hundred feet away Lyssa felt the intense, brutal heat.

"For God's sake, Bhuul!" she chided. "I said singe, not incinerate!"

The dragon lifted his head. "The cloak survives where her body shielded it," he observed. "Enough to be recognised at least."

She hurried back to look, and had to concede Bhuul was correct. The cloak was blackened and burned except for a woman shaped patch where its bright colours survived. Lyssa lifted the, now charred, body off the cloak and dragged it a few feet away. "Now I must be eaten," she murmured.

Bhuul lowered his head and picked up the body of the provisioner's daughter. He chewed thoughtfully. "Will they believe?"

"What is there not to believe?" Lyssa replied. "The wagon train was attacked. All were killed. Several horses have disappeared and two of the travellers with them, presumably all eaten by the attacking dragons. One of the two humans is Lyssa Gort, identified both by the wagon train's records and by her beautiful and distinctive riding cloak that lies burned where she fell. It will all seem so simple and obvious."

Bhuul swallowed. "I would not believe," he observed. "What dragon would eat you when there are horses available?"

"Trust me," Lyssa murmured, "no-one will even think to ask that question." Then she considered. "Well one, maybe, but with luck he'll not be here."

The dragon rumbled, a sound Lyssa … no, not 'Lyssa' any more, Lyssa was dead … a sound Khaajd felt more as a vibration running through her body than actually heard. "Well," he conceded, "you know humans. Now we must be gone. My companions and I will have been seen flying in, there are villages around here. Three in, so only three must leave. Come, Khaajd, I will carry you."

Reaching down Bhuul formed his huge, left-hand front talon into a tube. This he presented to Khaajd who climbed inside the cradle, lying across the fingers. The dragon climbed, three legged, up the mountainside to the top and launched himself into the air. His vast wings beating, he flew north. Normally he would have climbed above the mountain tops, but knowing he carried a human who could not survive in such thin air forced him to keep low, weaving between the peaks rather than passing over them. Half an hour he flew, long enough to be sure they were beyond the prying eyes of humans, then he dropped. Moments later Khaajd stood, once more, on solid ground.

"Now," Bhuul complained, "I grow weary of the whining voice of a human."

Khaajd gestured him away without a word. He gave her space, then turned to watch with vague curiosity as she removed her clothing and stood, naked, on the mountainside.

The change began.

At first it was a strange swelling of the body. Her limbs thickening and lengthening. Her chest getting deeper. Her neck stretched and her face distorted, growing longer. Khaajd gritted her teeth, for when massive changes occur in a body it is beyond hope that they would occur without pain. She hated changing. She hated it with a vengeance. Muscles burned with searing agony. Bones felt as if they were breaking and re-knitting a dozen times a minute.

She collapsed onto all fours, screaming a scream that was already deep and inhuman, tipping back a tormented head on a neck ten feet long, then twelve and growing by the second. Her skin hardened and darkened. The faint hint of scales appeared. From her back lumps sprouted just behind her already inhuman shoulder blades, spreading and growing into budding wings, wide and deep. Her hands extended, fingers becoming gnarled, and fingernails transforming into vicious, hooked, blue-black claws.

Again she tipped back her head and screamed. This time the sound was a bellow of agony, echoing between the mountains and accompanied by an involuntary blast of fire that jetted high into the mountain air. Then, as the change neared the end, the agony at last began to fade. She could breathe again, through lungs no longer tortured. The savage, searing pain that had burned through her dulled to an ache, more a thing of memory than of body. She collapsed onto the rock, both exhausted and relieved.

She spoke as a dragon. "The humans," she gasped, "have a legend of a place, a place of torment for the evil, a place called hell. I know hell, I go there every time I change."

Bhuul watched a few moments longer. "It didn't appear a pleasant experience," he observed. "Do you need rest?"

"Without doubt. I'll not be fit to fly for an hour at least. I must eat too, changing always leaves me famished."

"Thaakumek said I might need to hunt for you."

"She was right," Khaajd replied. "Five large goats, or eight small. Either would be most welcome."

"The queen's battle master must become goat catcher, it seems," Bhuul grumbled, but he turned his head down the slope and launched himself into the air.

For the next hour Bhuul scoured the nearby mountains for wild goats, snatching them off the steep slopes with his huge talons and dropping them to Khaajd. By the time she called that she had eaten enough she also felt stronger, able to crawl across the mountainside to find a steam from which she drank both long and deep. Another half hour and she was flapping her wings, feeling the muscles work. She still ached a little, but she was ready.

Hurling herself off the mountain she thrashed the air for a dozen strong beats to build up height and speed, then flapping less vigorously she gently circled and climbed to join Bhuul in the sky above. Together they turned for the very heart of the mountain range.

Up through the thin air she climbed, higher and higher, her breath streaming as intermittent blasts of white mist. The air howled beneath the beat of her wings and the mountains stretched out into the blue haze of distance in front of her. After so long, so very long, it was good to be a dragon again. Good to be Khaajd.

Higher and faster, higher and faster, the blue sky above darkening, deep and rich, as the air thinned. She felt ice collect around her nostrils as her warm, damp breath met the icy blast, but it was a delight to her. She allowed it to collect and then snorted it off, enjoying the caress of the fragments against her face and neck as the air whipped them away.

This was who she was! Not the tiny, insignificant, dark-haired girl she had been for so long. A dragon flying through the dragons' mountains. She was home at last. Faster she flew, driving her muscles to their limits, exhilarated by sensations so long denied.

Three miles behind and to one side Bhuul followed, the great battle dragon comfortably able to match any speed or height she could hope to achieve. For an hour they flew, a hundred and sixty leagues, far from the world of humans. By now the short winter day was drawing to a close, the sun dropped low to the west, yet there was still enough light for dragon eyes to see the land below.

A gleam caught Khaajd's eye. The shimmer of water. A lake caught in a bowl of the mountains. Beside the lake, lounging on the rocks, lay a dragon. Khaajd started to circle, drawing in her wings to 'stoop' like a hunting hawk. Down to the lake edge she swooped, cupping her wings and slowing until she dropped onto the stone beside the other dragon. They looked at each other.

Khaajd slightly spread her wings, pressing them to the ground. A gesture of respect to a senior. This was Thaakumek, queen of dragons.

"Welcome back, Khaajd." Thaakumek's eyes gleamed in the setting sun. "You have been away from us for too long."

The rock jumped as Bhuul landed nearby. Ripples danced across the surface of the lake.

"Far too long, Thaakumek," Khaajd agreed.

There was no concept of titles among dragons as there was among humans. Thaakumek might be called the queen of dragons, but not as a mark of respect. It was simply as a description of who she was. Dragons addressed other dragons by name, regardless of status. Respect and rank were expressed by gesture, such as Khaajd's 'wing press'.

Bhuul, in turn, wing pressed and waited. Watching and listening.

"So now you know all about humans?" Thaakumek asked. "You know of their ways and manners? You can pass among them without suspicion, one human among many?"

Khaajd considered her reply. "To know all is too great a claim for any one creature," she said, "yet I have learned much. I understand their kind perhaps as well as they understand themselves. I can talk as a human. Walk as a human. Live as a human."

"And <u>kill</u> as a human?"

"That would depend," Khaajd observed, "on what I am to kill."

"They kill <u>us</u>," the queen murmured. "When I was younger I believed we would have trouble with humankind. I suspected we would face crossbows, barbed spear traps and any number of other devices designed to slay us. Yet I always thought we would face these dangers in the margins of our range, the places where the high mountains give way to the green hills. Here ..." her head swivelled, her eyes scanning the landscape around her "... I thought we were safe, and always would be. Humans were lowland creatures, not creatures of the high peaks. They would stay where they belonged, and we would stay where we belonged, and the problem would be the few places where we overlapped. I believed we would have trouble from humans, but a <u>limited</u> trouble." Her eyes returned to Khaajd. "What a fool I was, naïve and stupid. Even when the truth began to appear I did not believe my own eyes, because what I saw didn't match what I believed I knew."

"You could not have see this coming!" Bhuul rumbled from the slope above.

Thaakumek turned to him. "My strongest battle dragon is also my strongest defender," she murmured, "even when he defends me from myself." She looked back to Khaajd. "Yet for all his defence I misunderstood the humans. Where I feared crossbows and spear traps they are killing us with other weapons. Weapons more lethal, more brutal, more merciless by far. They are killing us with <u>cities</u>."

Khaajd's neck straightened. "Cities?"

"First they build a city," Thaakumek explained. "They build it with great walls and towers. Defences that seem impervious to dragon fire, but unleash a hissing cloud of crossbow bolts. A city we

27

cannot break, one we cannot destroy. Then, when the city is secure, humans move in. Roads spread in all directions. Twenty, thirty, forty leagues or more. Along these roads flow humans, and beside them appear towns and villages, workshops and mines. The humans fill the air with filth so it smells evil. They fill the streams and lakes with filth so they taste evil. They drive away the goats and other mountain creatures that we hunt. Then we starve. In ones. In tens. In hundreds. Almost before we know what has happened a great expanse of our mountains has gone. We cannot live there any more, for there is nothing to eat. Then, having done ... they build another city."

"And now, having grown more confident," Bhuul added, "they build cities two at a time."

"We are losing our mountains, Khaajd," Thaakumek said. "Not just the edges, the margins, we are losing everything. City by city, town by town, road by road, it is all being taken from us. Even the deepest parts of the range, where the mountains are highest and the air is freshest, are doomed. Look!" She jabbed her nose in one direction. "Over there is my cave. And there ..." her head turned "... is my favourite hunting ground. There are no humans within a hundred leagues, but for how long? When will I smell smoke? When will I taste a taint in my lake? When will I lie, starving and dying, on the mountainside, too weak to fly? Fifty years? A hundred?" Her voice dropped almost to nothing. "It will not be much longer."

"This is not your fault," Bhuul growled.

"But it is my responsibility," Thaakumek replied. "I am queen of my people, and my people deserve an answer from their queen. I fly the mountains and see fear in dragon eyes. Despair. The humans will take away their food, their water, their homes, their pride ... and their hope. Then, when they have nothing else to lose, the humans will take their lives. They know it! There is nothing I would not do to save my people, Khaajd. If fighting would save them I would bite until I could no longer snap my jaws, I would flame until I had no breath left, I would fly until my wings collapsed under me. Yet there is nothing I can do. Nothing. I have no answer. Why do these humans hate us so?"

"They don't," Khaajd murmured. "For sure they feel aggrieved when dragons attack human villages and wagon trains, killing the people, but for the most part they hardly think of dragons at all. They just live their lives. They are ruled by a man named Telchar Bliss, a 'duke' as you are a queen. I have not met the duke, but some days ago I met a close friend and aid of his called Farron. Farron told me that dragons are merely an 'inconvenience'. He seemed almost amused when it was suggested we might be a genuine threat."

For a dozen seconds Thaakumek said nothing, then when her voice came it burned with bitterness. "And so I am told of my insignificance, and that of my people. An inconvenience alone, not even capable of earning the hatred of those who kill us." She closed her eyes. Her head drooped towards the rock. "What is it that these humans dig from the mountains? What to they need so much that my people must starve?"

"Copper." Khaajd replied. "Tin. Coal. Iron. Silver and gold. Gemstones."

Thaakumek's head tilted slightly. "Gemstones?"

Khaajd fashioned a definition. "Pretty rocks."

That, too, took some seconds to digest. "My people must die for pretty rocks?"

How could Khaajd answer? She took a deep breath. "Not only for pretty rocks but, yes, for them among other things."

"Why?" It was only a single word, but filled with so many things. Pain. Despair. Shock. Horror. Bewilderment.

"Because humans are not like us," Khaajd said. "Give a dragon a promise of good food, clean water, a sheltered cave and the health of his body, and he will be happy. He will fly through the mountains with joy in his heart. Give a human the exact same but no more, and he will be wretched. Humans seek happiness through <u>things</u>. Things they own. Things they possess. Things they control. To feel content in life a man must have clothes, and shoes, and gold, and cattle, and a house, and furniture, and tools, and armour, and a sword, and gems ... and ... and ... and ...! A man that owns ten things burns to own ten more. A man who owns ten thousand seeks <u>another</u> ten thousand. That is the way of mankind."

"So even when all the dragons are dead, and every pretty rock has been cut from the mountains, that will <u>still</u> not be enough?"

"Not if every pretty rock became a thousand would it be enough," Khaajd replied. "The human hunger to own things is never satisfied. The more things they own, the stronger their desire to own more."

"Then they will never stop." Thaakumek's voice almost disappeared. "If they believe there are things to be dug from the mountains they will always dig."

"Unless we can find a way to stop them," murmured Khaajd.

"You think we haven't tried?" It was Bhuul. "I have lead the battle dragons against the cities using every strategy I could devise. We fought by day, or by night. We overflew them to drop rocks, or attacked on foot with tooth, flame and claw. We struck hard with everything we had, or harboured our forces so we could maintain the pressure for days. We concentrated our efforts in one place, or attacked the whole city. Whatever we did the result was always the same. Strong battle dragons died, and the cities remained."

"And then?" Khaajd asked.

"Then I tried a different approach," Bhuul continued. "Instead of leading dragons against the cities I turned against the towns, villages and mines. There the humans have no lethal, dragon-killing defences. Instead they dig chambers deep into the mountain rock. Chambers in which they hide when we attack. Chambers which keep them safe and out of our reach. If we attack suddenly and without warning we can sometimes kill a few before they are able to flee, but in truth all we achieve is the destruction of the buildings. We smash everything that can be smashed. We flame everything that can be flamed. We leave nothing standing taller than a tall goat, but as soon as we are gone the humans climb out of their holes and start to re-build. Six months later it is as if we had never been there."

"Bhuul's efforts, heroic as they have been, have all failed," Thaakumek confirmed. "Whatever he has tried we simply cannot kill enough humans or do enough damage to make them go away."

"Yet now you have a new weapon, Thaakumek," Khaajd observed. "You have a dragon who can walk as a human among humans. I will go to one of their cities. I will see what no dragon has ever seen before. I will hear what no dragon has ever heard before. I will <u>learn</u> what no dragon has ever <u>learned</u> before! From inside the city itself I shall discover its weakness and find how it may be destroyed. This I promise, or I shall die in the attempt."

Thaakumek considered these words. "If the humans recognise you for what you are," she said, "they will kill you. As a human you will have no chance of escape. Deep within the city there will be no chance of us saving you. You will be on your own among ten thousand enemies. I cannot command this of you, it is too much."

"You do not have to command," Khaajd said. "I have no choice."

"No choice?"

"When I first went to live among humans," Khaajd explained, "I was bewildered. The way they thought, the way they acted and what they desired were all alien to me. I found them beyond my understanding and, doubtless, they found me exactly the same. Yet, as the first few years passed, I started to understand them better. Their ways were still alien to me, but at least I could <u>pretend</u> to be as they were. As more years passed the pretence got easier. More natural. More instinctive. More years still and I had changed. Without even realising it I drifted from being a dragon who pretended to be a human, into being a human. To my shame I actually forgot who I really was. Then ..." Thaakumek could hear the sudden pain in her voice "... something happened that reminded me."

"I know of that something." Thaakumek reached out to nuzzle Khaajd behind her right ear flap. "I am truly sorry for your loss."

"When I stood beside my mothers head," Khaajd said, "knowing how she had suffered and how she had died, I felt a traitor. I should have known, but I didn't trouble myself to look. I should have helped, but I failed her. Never again! Never! I am a dragon, not a human. I failed my mother but I will not fail my queen or my people. I just ... can't."

"I cannot command you in this," Thaakumek repeated, "but if you will do it, for me and for our people, I will be grateful to you for as long as I live. Whatever may come of your efforts."

"Then it will be done," Khaajd said. "I will go to the human city called Tekmir. It is not the largest of their cities, not any more, but it was the first of them. The one from which the others were copied. It would be ... fitting ... that the first city built should be the first to fall."

Thaakumek looked at her for a full thirty seconds. "But not yet, Khaajd," she said. "Not yet. For a few days at least you must be a dragon in the dragons' mountains. Until you return to humankind my cave is your cave, my hunting grounds are your hunting grounds, my lake is your lake. Eat and sleep and breathe the fresh air, and Khaajd ...?"

"Yes ...?"

"Thank you."

# Chapter Three

---

Khaajd spent a little over a week as a dragon. She hunted in the mountains. She bathed in deep, ice-cold pools. She flew high and long and far, while the world beneath her slipped silently by. At night she slept in the open, under crystal stars and an ink-black sky.

She had almost forgotten what clean air was. Living in village and town she had grown used to breathing air tainted with the scents of human life. With smoke and sweat, food and refuse, beast and dung. Now, at last, she could fill her lungs with purity. With air so clean, so untouched, that it almost sparkled in the cold, winter sunshine. It was a time of absolute, unlimited bliss. Or would have been, but for anticipation.

She knew the sound that would herald her ejection from this temporary paradise. Even while she basked and bathed and slept she unconsciously listened for it.

Then she heard it.

Whoosh … whoosh … whoosh.

The beating of wings. Faint at first, but getting closer. Nearer.

She was lying in Thaakumek's lake, water barely above freezing merely refreshing for a creature of her size and thickness of hide. Her neck was stretched out on the rocks at the lake edge. Her eyes were closed. She hovered in that undefined place that is neither sleep nor true wakefulness.

Slowly the sound permeated her consciousness. Whoosh … whoosh … whoosh.

She willed it away. She willed herself fully asleep.

Whoosh … whoosh … whoosh. Close now, and the sound changed. Gone was the beat of wings, to be replaced by the steady but growing roar of gliding descent. Closer. Closer. She felt the ground jump. Heard the clatter of claw on stone. The crunch of a talon closing to grip. The dry, crisp rasp of scale on rock.

Then silence. Half a minute of complete silence.

"You look peaceful, Khaajd." It was Thaakumek, of course. "It seems almost a pity to disturb you."

Khaajd emitted the deepest rumble of discontent. Tiny ripples ran across the surface of the lake. Even with her eyes closed she could imagine Thaakumek tongue wrapping in amusement. More sounds of movement, and she felt the nuzzle of a dragon's nose. Warm breath flowed over her.

She opened her eyes to find the dragon queen looking intently at her. "Time to become a human again?"

"If you are still willing to go to Tekmir for us."

"I am." Khaajd allowed herself a few more seconds of indulgence and then hauled herself out of the water. "Time to become Lyssa once more."

Thaakumek's head tilted. "Lyssa? Isn't she dead?"

"There are millions of humans," Khaajd explained, "and only a limited number of names for them. Lyssa is a fairly common name, so there are many Lyssas walking the world. I shall simply return as another one."

"And this is an advantage?"

"It means I am less likely to use the wrong name in a moment's lack of concentration," Khaajd said. "It certainly made it easier the last time I died and returned."

The queen's head tilted a fraction further. "You've done this before?"

"Humans live about sixty years," Khaajd explained. "We live, maybe, twelve hundred. In one decade they age as much as I would in two centuries, so every ten or so years I have to die and return as someone much younger before the humans notice I'm not getting older as I should. So far I've died twice."

Thaakumek looked thoughtful. "So this will be the third Lyssa."

"Indeed," Khaajd confirmed. "The first, Lyssa Brottoss, was a simple, country girl. In truth I didn't know enough to pretend to be anything else. She drowned a little over ten years ago when a freak wave swept her out to sea."

"Unfortunate," Thaakumek murmured.

"The second," continued Khaajd, "was Lyssa Gort. She was something of an adventuress to travelled widely, trading in metals and metal ores. She was, in theory, thirty-two when she was eaten by Bhuul but looked like a woman of twenty. Even if Bhuul hadn't eaten her she would have had to die soon in some other way."

"And the third manifestation?" Thaakumek asked. "The new one?"

"The new Lyssa must be able to discover things without suspicion," Khaajd said. "She must be a pretty thing who can use her wiles to coax indiscretions from the Tekmiri soldiers. A girl who can ask important questions and make them sound innocent. She will wear fine dresses and delicate shoes. She will coil her hair high on her head in the latest styles, and artfully colour her face ..."

"Colour her face?" Thaakumek's astonishment tore the words from her.

Khaajd tongue wrapped. "Humans do that," she said. "Mainly human females, it must be said, but not exclusively so. They colour their faces with pigments to enhance their attractiveness."

The concept was utterly bizarre to the dragon queen. "Enhance their attractiveness? By making their faces different colours?"

"Parts of their faces."

Thaakumek considered the idea, astonished. "And you did this when you were a human female?"

"Not in my first manifestation," Khaajd said. "Lyssa Brottoss was an unsophisticated girl. As Lyssa Gort I did, on occasion, but not often as it was not really my style."

Thaakumek considered the matter, and then consciously pushed it aside. "I set Bhuul a task over the last week," she announced. "He took half a dozen battle dragons and attacked every town, village and wagon train he could. Wherever they attacked they took everything they could carry, and brought it back to my cave. There it remains. I have no idea what they collected, I know nothing of human things. Neither do the battle dragons. I hope, though, that you will find useful items. It will be good to send you back to the human world better prepared than we managed the first time."

"I shall look," Khaajd said, "and see what I can find." Of course the idea of returning to the human world also meant she would have to face the hell of changing form. "I shall need to rest, eat and stay warm after I change."

"My cave is yours," Thaakumek said. "I will personally hunt you a goat, collect firewood, light it and lie in the cave mouth to block out the wind. You are the one weapon we have against the humans, and I will take the best care of you."

Together the two dragons made their way to Thaakumek's cave. Her home. In the back of the cave Khaajd found a vast stack of all sorts of things that she, alone among dragons, recognised and understood. There were containers of all sorts. Sacks, saddle bags, cases and trunks were everywhere. Then there were other things. Shattered furniture from shattered houses. Wardrobes, chests, cupboards and bookcases lay in broken heaps, their former contents spilled on the cave floor. Then oddities, things taken by dragons that had no idea of what they were. A couple of wood burning stoves, their thin, metal chimneys buckled and torn off. Two beds and at least five chairs, all smashed. A small donkey cart. To one side a workshop bench teetered on three legs with a hatchet, part sharpened, still fastened in its vice.

"Do you think you'll find what you need?" Thaakumek asked.

Khaajd looked at the vast pile of ... things ... in front of her. "Probably. There are containers here that are intended to hold clothes. Others that might contain coin. Others where I may find tools. I shall have to search ..."

She suddenly stopped. Thaakumek noticed the hesitation. "Is there something wrong?"

"No." Khaajd's voice was suddenly quiet. "Not wrong. I've just seen something."

"Tell me."

Khaajd prodded with her nose. "That," she said. "It's a crib. A sort of ... movable cave ... that humans make for their children. A place they can feel warm and safe as they sleep. Seeing it makes me wonder ..." She fell silent.

"... if the young human who slept in it still lives?" Thaakumek completed the thought. "It is possible. As Bhuul said, the humans of the towns and villages have underground chambers they flee to when dragons attack. If the young one was taken to such a chamber he may have survived."

"I hope so," Khaajd murmured. "I know humans are the enemy of our people, but somehow it would be a shame for a child to die. A child who had not yet learned what dragons are, let alone learned to hate us."

Thaakumek considered these words. "That I can understand," she said, "yet there will be young ones in Tekmir, the city you are planning to help us destroy. If you succeed they are doomed. If you succeed all the humans in the city are doomed."

"I know," Khaajd murmured. "Discovering how to destroy Tekmir will be hard, but it will not be the only thing I shall find difficult. Yes, I will feel regret but you need not be concerned. My mind is sure even if my heart may ache at times."

"I can ask no more," Thaakumek said. "Neither can your people."

The queen of dragons made good her promise. She personally caught Khaajd a goat and brought it to her cave. She didn't, as it happened, need to collect firewood as there was a vast supply of smashed furniture which would supply all the fuel Khaajd could need. Like Bhuul before her she watched, fascinated, as Khaajd underwent the agony of transformation, becoming once more a pale skinned girl with long, dark hair.

Famished and exhausted, with every muscle aching, Khaajd set her own priorities. Taking the half sharp hatchet from the work bench she smashed open boxes and furniture until she found enough clothing to protect her from a cold she hadn't felt as a dragon, but now felt intensely as a human.

Next came warmth. Dragon breath was too potent to unleash within the cave, so Thaakumek dragged the child's crib outside and snorted it alight while Khaajd split furniture and built a fire. She then transferred flame from outside to inside and added more fuel until she had built a large, comforting blaze.

Then came food. She searched for a knife and then used it to crudely butcher the goat. She cut strips of fresh meat and skewered them on spikes of broken furniture so she could roast them before the flames. Thaakumek's green eyes watched this bizarre activity with bewildered curiosity. She wrinkled her nose at the smell of the cooking meat.

Khaajd ate voraciously. True, fire roasted goat wasn't exactly the finest fare, but when famished to the point of near collapse that hardly mattered. Goat meat would do. Once she had taken the edge off her own hunger she offered a skewer of cooked goat to Thaakumek. The dragon queen wrinkled her nose, declining the offer. She was astonished that any sane creature would take perfectly good goat and sear it over flame before eating it.

Finally came the desperate need for sleep. She built up the fire as high as she could, took a mattress from one of the broken beds, and fell upon it. She was asleep almost before she lay down. For the whole night Thaakumek lay in the cave mouth, a living wind break and door to keep the winter chill out.

The next morning, when properly rested and fully recovered from the change, she ate a second meal of goat and made a more careful search of the gathered items. There were many clothes suitable for a young woman. There were combs for her hair, belts and pouches and plenty of coin to go in them. There were sturdy boots and delicate shoes, though she had to make a careful search to find a fit. There was jewellery that she could later sell to further bolster her funds. For her belt she found a long, fine lady's dagger. She hoped she would never have to use it, but it was a comfort to hang it at her waist. She would most certainly be returning to the human world better equipped than she had been the first time. By mid morning she had ransacked the collection as best she could, and nothing more was to be had from it.

"So how do we get you to Tekmir?" Thaakumek asked.

Khaajd considered. "You don't," she replied. "A human woman would not travel through the mountains alone and unmounted, so if I appeared at Tekmir's gates on foot I would attract far more interest than I should. Questions would be asked and answers expected. Take me, instead, to the edge of the mountains. Somewhere I can walk out into the lowlands and find a village. I'll then buy a horse and make my own way to Tekmir the way a woman should."

"That I can arrange."

So Khaajd returned to the human world by the darkening light of late evening. She travelled the way she had left it, a passenger in the loop of Bhuul's left claw. The battle dragon took her right to the edge of the mountains. There he circled and scouted for a suitable place where he could land and deposit his charge unseen.

"There is a road a short way over there," Bhuul pointed with his nose to indicate direction, "that leads some five miles to a small, human town. A fair walk for one so small, but I could not carry you closer without the risk of being seen."

Lyssa, as she now was again, nodded. "Five miles I can cope with. More importantly, how do I contact you when I'm in Tekmir?"

"I have, with my battle dragons, established a position close to the city from where we watch it," he said. "The humans are aware we're there. They could hardly not be, we perch on a mountain top in full view some ten miles from their walls. If you can approach our watch mountain without being seen then you can speak to the dragon there. Sometimes me, but sometimes one of my trusted lieutenants."

"Or be eaten by him," Lyssa laughed.

"I shall instruct the watch dragons to check before harming any lone human that approaches," Bhuul assured her. "The difficulty will be approaching the place unnoticed."

"Difficult, possibly," Lyssa mused, "but not impossible. The humans of Tekmir see dragons as dangerous creatures, they will not be greatly concerned what a single, human girl does."

"Their lack of vision will be their downfall if you manage to find the way to destroy them," Bhuul observed, "but that is for the future. I shall await further news with interest. When might you learn something of use?"

"How should I know?" Lyssa asked. "I cannot plan when someone might say something foolish to me, or when inspiration might strike. You have waited over twenty years since last attacking Tekmir, perhaps you will have to wait some while longer."

Bhuul considered. "A fair point," he conceded. "As long as the end result is the desired one I can maintain my patience waiting for it."

"It will be," she assured him. "I have given my promise to Thaakumek."

"Promises can sometimes be impossible to keep," Bhuul rumbled. "I have failed in some of my own regarding the human cities."

For several seconds Lyssa looked into the dragon's eyes. "Not failed, Bhuul," she said, "just not succeeded yet."

With those words she left Bhuul and headed off by foot to find her way back to the human world. Five miles was some way and she was walking into the dark of night, yet this didn't particularly concern her. She did not fear the dark, which was reasonable. Nor did she fear that which could lurk in the dark, which was somewhat less justified but caused her no problem on this occasion.

The stars were already bright overhead when she saw the lights of civilisation ahead of her. She had never been to this town before, but these mountain edge towns tended to be much the same. There would be homes, houses, at least one stable, at least one inn and workshops.

The first priority was a horse. It would be bizarre indeed for a young woman to arrive at an inn unannounced, unexpected and late into the night with no obvious means of having travelled there. The last thing she wanted was to arouse curiosity. She needed a horse, merely as a prop. She headed for the stables.

Despite the lateness of the hour she managed to rouse a stable-lad, and via him the owner of the stable. To state the owner was sceptical about a young woman seeking to buy a horse at this hour understated the fact, but the glitter of coin appeared to make his misgivings evaporate as if by sorcery. Gold was truly a substance of magic among humankind.

Within half an hour the transaction was done and Lyssa was the proud owner of a new horse and the necessary tack to ride him. Not a fine beast by any measure, but fair and functional. The horse's first duty was to carry his new owner barely five hundred yards to the inn, where Lyssa dismounted with a show of tiredness appropriate for a long day in the saddle. Tying her mount she made her way inside and sought out the innkeeper.

Like the stable owner before him she saw the scepticism in his eyes. A woman travelling alone was a rarity. One travelling in these troubled times, with dragon attacks nearby, was rarer still. That the woman was obviously both young and beautiful made her rarest of all.

Lyssa chose to address his doubts directly, so that she could do so in her own way. "Don't ask!" she laughed. "Let's just say there is a young man who I have a burning desire to strangle."

The man grinned, his eyes softening. "Ah!" His voice took on a knowing tone. "Perhaps best to leave the matter at that?"

"I would be most obliged," Lyssa murmured.

"Then I shall say no more. Your horse is …?"

"Just outside," she told him. "Tethered to the post at your door."

"I shall have one of the lads see to him," the innkeeper said. "A stall, straw, water and oats?"

"That would be excellent," Lyssa confirmed, "and for me a room, a meal, some fine wine and, if you would oblige, some local information." She saw his hesitation. A young woman, however comely, who had been left in need of a room by unfortunate circumstance might also have been left in need of funds. She grinned. "I shall, of course, pay for all in advance." She placed a golden coin called a 'wheel' on the counter.

Once more the glitter of gold had the miraculous effect of banishing misgivings. "Of course! How can I help you, madam?"

"I must return to Tekmir," she said, "but I understand at least one wagon train has been attacked by dragons of late."

"Three," the innkeeper corrected. "Indeed there has been more trouble with dragons than we've had for many a year. The last week in particular there seems to have been a band of them striking at anything they can find."

"So do the wagon trains still run?"

"Well, y-e-e-e-s," he sounded unsure, "but less frequent and vastly more expensive. The warriors guarding them demand higher fees now, in light of the increased danger."

Lyssa nodded. "That I can understand," she said. "If I were such a warrior I, too, would only want to take great risks if I could become genuinely rich doing so. Yet if coin is available passage can still be bought?"

"Indeed," the innkeeper confirmed. "Unfortunately you will need to wait some time to do so. We're not expecting the train back from Tekmir for three or four more days."

Lyssa shrugged. "Then it would appear, sir, that you have a guest for that time. Perhaps I should leave both that wheel, and another, on account. You can then either ask for more or return change as appropriate in the days to come."

"That would be <u>most</u> satisfactory, madam," he beamed at her.

Her horse was taken to the inn stables, and Lyssa shown to her room. She ate and made herself comfortable while she waited for the wagon train to return. Having established for the innkeeper's benefit that there was some 'trouble' involved in her sudden appearance, probably in the form of a lovers' tiff, he was discrete enough to ask no more. Exactly as Lyssa had intended when telling the tale.

For three days Lyssa availed herself of the local shops, buying clothing that fitted her better than the items found at random among the broken acquisitions of dragon attack. She also bought cosmetics to colour her face in sophisticated style, and grips to hold her coiled hair in place. Back in her room she experimented with her new purchases and was rather delighted to find a distinctly pretty, feminine girl gazing at her from the mirror. The new Lyssa was truly born.

"That will do," she murmured to herself.

By the time the wagon train returned she was ready for it, and for the second time she rode into a market square in the cold of pre-dawn. This time, though, the atmosphere among the soldiers was as icy as the winter weather. They were scared, there was no other word for it. The gathered travellers also seemed remarkably few in number.

As before there was a make-shift table and a captain sitting behind it. She made her way to him. "One rider, one horse for Tekmir," she announced.

The man looked up at her. His words were of warning. "You are aware, miss, that there are considerable dangers in this journey? Three trains have recently been attacked by dragons, and all in them slain?"

Lyssa nodded. "I am aware," she replied, "but sometimes necessity overrides caution."

He nodded. "Then your need must be great," he said. "I hope the weight of your purse matches it. My men are not prepared to face the threat of dragons for meagre reward, and rightly so. Neither am I. The fee is four golden wheels per person and four more per beast."

A wheel had the value of twenty silver crowns, so the passage to Tekmir had increased in price forty-fold in a couple of weeks. Lyssa allowed herself a raised eyebrow. "I don't suppose it would serve any useful purpose to claim that price is excessive?"

"None whatever," the captain assured her. "You may take it or leave it as you wish, miss ..." he paused, looking at her a little more intensely "... though perhaps if the sum were truly a problem for you then some other ... arrangement ... might be possible."

She reached into her belt pouch, extracted eight golden wheels, and tossed them onto the table. "No other arrangement will be either required or welcome, Captain."

He looked at the coins scattered on the desk top, then back up at her. An impish grin appeared on his face. "Pity," he chuckled. "Still, miss, the gold will serve as a fine compensation indeed. There will not be many travelling with us. Few have the determination, courage and need."

"Or the funds, perhaps," Lyssa added.

"That too," the captain added. "Those that are travelling are gathered over there." He indicated with a nod. "Please join them."

Again Lyssa raised an eyebrow.

"No signing of the book?" she asked. "No detailing the next of kin to be informed in the case of misfortune?"

"To what purpose?" the captain asked. "If the dragons attack I doubt the contents of my register will still be readable after being bathed in flame."

"Besides," Lyssa observed, "when you are charging four golden wheels per person or beast, perhaps it is best not to have that noted in a physical record?"

He chuckled. "There is also that."

The actual journey to Tekmir proved about as uneventful as a journey could be, to the great relief of all and the expectation of Lyssa alone. Bhuul, of course, knew where he had left her, and that she would be travelling from there to Tekmir, so he make sure no wagon trains in that area were attacked. In fact dragon attacks in general were getting less frequent now that their purpose of providing Lyssa with useful human items was complete. All Bhuul now did was ensure there was no sudden cessation of aggression which might have aroused questions. Instead he allowed the attacks to fade away over the next couple of weeks. Lyssa, therefore, approached the main gates of Tekmir considerably lighter in gold but without other incident, except for the occasional obscene suggestion from the escorting soldiers.

Tekmir was not a huge place by comparison with the vast lowland cities. It wasn't even the biggest of the mountain cities, Yullat had a population several times as great, yet it was still a substantial place of some sixty thousand people. Of those sixty thousand at least one in ten were soldiers employed to man the anti-dragon defences, a huge expense that could only be justified by the vast fortune that flowed through the city's streets, courtesy of the surrounding multitude of mines. Ultimately, then, Tekmir was a hub for the mining industry. A place of merchants in metals, gems, supplies, liquor, tools, clothing and all the other needs of the mining industry. Accompanying the legitimate trades were those less legitimate. Those that always appear in places where gold is both quickly earned and quickly spent. Tekmir's night-time streets were filled with prostitution, narcotics, gambling and crime.

A place where fortunes could be made, at a risk and a price.

For Lyssa, however, this was of little interest. As she rode the final mile to the city she found herself looking intently, and for the first time, at the great walls that surrounded the place. Or, more specifically, at the tops of those walls. There were the defences designed specifically to guard against a particular enemy, dragons.

Topping the walls were things called 'galleries', very different from the battlements you would expect if humans were the anticipated foe. Yet from ground level they looked remarkably unremarkable, the walls just seemed topped by a brown building with long windows and many chimneys. There was nothing to indicate why these walls posed the lethal danger to attacking dragons that she knew them to be.

As well as the outer walls there were, dotted throughout the city, tall 'dragon towers'. These were topped with a structure similar to the wall-top galleries, again brown in colour with the same windows and multitude of chimneys.

By the time the wagon train arrived at the city gate her head was already filled with questions for which she had no answers.

"Miss ...?"

Somehow she had to get inside one of the galleries or tower caps to see what they contained. She had to understand.

"Miss ...?"

47

She returned to the moment. "My apologies, sir," she said to the gate guard who had been trying to attract her attention. "My mind was on other matters."

"No problem, miss." The man grinned with good humour. "I just need your name for the records."

Lyssa hesitated just long enough to to ensure she spoke her latest surname rather than either of the earlier two. "Name? Of course. Lyssa Urdak."

"Lyssa Urdak." He made a note of the name in a small register. "And your purpose in coming to Tekmir?"

"Business. I trade in cloth and cloth goods."

Again he noted. "Excellent. And where will you be staying, Miss Urdak?"

She smiled. "At an inn, yet to be chosen," she said, "which brings me to a question. If I was seeking such an inn, one where the food was good and the rooms clean, would you be able to recommend one?"

The guard considered. "There are two that spring to mind, miss," he said, "though which would be the better for you would depend on your budget."

Lyssa smiled. "That is not a problem."

"Then you could do no better than the 'Dragon's Fall' off Temple Square."

Lyssa frowned. "Something of a strange name, surely?"

The man laughed. "There used to be a warehouse there," he explained, "but during a dragon attack some fifty years ago one of the attacking dragons was slain and literally fell on top of it. It was utterly crushed. The land was cleared and the inn built, its name honouring the event."

"Indeed." Lyssa said dryly. "So how do I find the Dragon's Fall?"

"Go straight up the main road from this gate for five hundred yards or so," the soldier directed. "You'll come to a cross roads decorated with a statue of a warrior with sword and shield. Turn right and another two hundred yards will take you to Temple Square. The temple opens onto the north of the square, the inn is to the south. You can't miss it."

She nodded and, the formalities at the gate over, made her way to the Dragon's Fall. It seemed strange to her, a dragon going to stay at an inn named in honour of the death of a dragon, yet in another way it was appropriate. The fallen dragon would be avenged and the inn that celebrated his death would be destroyed.

These thoughts aside she could not help but find the inn pleasant indeed. The common room was clean, brightly lit, delightfully decorated and filled with the sound of merriment and the smell of good food. The innkeeper was both charming and welcoming and, when she had offered initial payment on account, showed her to a room that was little short of luxurious. Yes, the cost was high, but due to Bhuul's efforts she had no shortage of funds.

There was also another advantage. As she had walked through the common room she had spotted soldiers in the livery of the city guard, and not common soldiers either. This inn was too expensive for the ordinary men, but was instead a favourite haunt of the officers.

Useful. In her room she spent some time washing, drying and combing her hair. She selected a dress, not overly elaborate but still one which showed her figure and flowed sleekly to her ankles. She swept her hair high on her head, delicately adorned her face with careful colour and returned to the common room.

The innkeeper saw her and approached. "Are you settled in, miss?"

"Very comfortably," she replied, "and now needing something pleasant to eat, if that can be arranged."

"Of course it can." He gestured her to a table. "We have a roast pig on the spit with vegetables and roasted potatoes to accompany. We have fine wines, meads, beers and ciders to drink. Applejack if you prefer something stronger, or various juices if that would serve you better. Alternatively our cook can prepare most dishes to order if there is something else you would like."

"The roasted pig, vegetables and potatoes sound perfect to me," she assured him. "My tastes are not greatly sophisticated, and as long as the food is good I shall eat it with great pleasure."

"Then you shall eat with pleasure," he assured her.

She sat and waited, both for the food and for something else. The something else came first.

"Good evening, miss."

She turned and found herself looking at a young guards officer. Behind him one of his colleagues called. "Brennar! Leave the poor girl alone! Can't she eat a meal in peace without you pouncing?"

Brennar glanced over his shoulder, then back to Lyssa. "If I have indeed 'pounced'," he grinned, "you have my apologies. However it was not my intention to offend, just to greet you and bid you welcome."

She smiled. "Your welcome has been both gentlemanly and polite," she assured him, "and not the merest hint of a pounce." He fractionally tilted his head, his eyes bright. "Alright," she corrected, "perhaps a <u>slight</u> pounce, but not to excess."

He laughed. "Good! I wouldn't want to have <u>completely</u> lost my skill for pouncing. I have something of a reputation for it, I fear, but I assure you it's a talent I reserve for the very prettiest of girls."

Lyssa raised an eyebrow. "And do you also have a reputation for flattery?"

"Guilty as charged."

Lyssa laughed. "Then while we are on the subject of faults admitted," she said, "vanity is one of mine."

"Excellent!" Brennar grinned. "Flattery and vanity are complimentary faults, fitting each other well." He indicated another chair at Lyssa's table. "May I join you, or would you prefer to eat alone?"

Lyssa nodded in acquiescence. "Company would be most pleasant," she said, "though I give you warning. Conversation might be somewhat lacking when my food arrives. I am hungry indeed."

He sat. "My name is Brennar, miss. Mardan Brennar, though I'm mostly known and addressed by my family name. I am a Lieutenant of Guard in this city." He held out his hand.

"I am Lyssa Urdak," Lyssa replied, reaching to delicately brush his fingers with her own. "Lyssa to my friends, and to you if you wish, Lieutenant."

He smiled. "I most certainly wish," he said. "Are you newly arrived in the city?"

"I have been here before," she said, "so not a complete stranger, but I have not spent long here before."

Brennar nodded. "So is your visit business or pleasure?"

She laughed. "<u>Officially</u> business. Cloth and clothing."

Cloth and clothing were not a subject of particular interest to the Lieutenant of Guard, much to Lyssa's relief as she actually knew little about the subject. He nodded and turned the subject to the matter that was closer to his own heart. "I hope not <u>all</u> of your time will be occupied with work?"

"Certainly not!" Lyssa laughed. "Next to vanity my second major fault is laziness."

"Excellent," he grinned. "Then maybe I shall have the opportunity to see more of you during your periods of leisure."

"Seeing more of me," Lyssa noted, "is a phrase open to two interpretations," the mischievous grin on his lips informed her that he, too, was aware of both, "only one of which is likely to happen."

The grin turned into laughter. "Which one, I wonder?"

"The one you least prefer, Lieutenant of Guard," she said.

He shrugged. "Damn. Then I shall still enjoy the more that I do see."

With that they were interrupted by the arrival of Lyssa's meal.

# Chapter Four

---

The work of a spy can sometimes be astonishingly easy, particularly if the spied upon doesn't see their own kind as a threat. During her meal Lyssa and Brennar spoke of trivialities, but as was almost inevitable this lead to to the main topic of conversation in the city those days, the recent spate of dragon attacks. From this it was easy for Lyssa to express nervousness about dragons, for Brennar to reassure her that there was no danger while she was in Tekmir, and for her to ask how he could be so sure.

Before she had eaten her final mouthful Brennar had invited her to visit Dragon Tower 17 with him the very next morning, so she could see for herself why the city was safe from attack. She pushed aside feelings of guilt at abusing the trust of a man who sought to reassure her. Her people were at war with his, and she had to fight using any weapon at her disposal. The meal finished she thanked the charming Lieutenant of Guard for his company, made her arrangements to meet him the next morning, and retired to her room for the night.

The next morning she rose early, washed, dressed in a close fitting shirt and breeches that showed her figure to good effect, swept her hair high and coloured her face. Whatever else she may do today, she would play the role of innocent but fascinated girl. After a hearty breakfast she awaited the arrival of her escort, who appeared with military precision at precisely the moment agreed. Together they walked to Tower 17.

The dragon towers were tall buildings and, for nine tenths of their height, remarkably uninteresting. Even to Lyssa. They entered through a steel door at the base and looked around. There was practically nothing to see.

"This bit's boring," grinned Brennar, echoing Lyssa's own view. "The bottom of the tower is just brick though, admittedly, thick brick to make it hard for the dragons to topple. The walls here ..." he patted the nearest one "... are almost nine feet. The outer two or three courses are the hot-fired bricks you find lining furnaces and kilns so they can withstand anything the dragons can breath at them. Inside that we use ordinary house bricks. In fact the bottom of the tower does nothing except provide storage and support the cap at the top."

They started climbing spiral stairs up the middle of the tower. Around them were rooms.

"There are no windows here," Brennar explained. "Nothing that would allow dragon fire in. The tower is lit by lamps all the time."

"And yet, surely, with many burning oil lamps and many soldiers breathing you'll need lots of fresh air."

Brennar paused as he climbed, turning to glance at her. It was an excellent point, and one which made him realise this pretty girl was not just a pretty girl. She had a brain as well. "We do," he agreed. "There are ducts at the bottom of the tower that lead into what we call the cellar. It's a large, underground space that acts as a flame trap so dragon fire cannot pass through it and into the tower. The cellar connects to the outside via other ducts and grills. At the top of the tower is a tall chimney with a large fire at the bottom. The heated air rises up the chimney and, in doing so, draws fresh air through the tower from bottom to top. As long as the fire burns there's a constant flow, and all of us breathe comfortably."

"Ah!" That made sense. "I had noticed the chimneys at the tops of the towers and galleries."

Brennar grinned. "There are two sorts of chimneys," he added, "that serve two different purposes. I'll explain the other when we get up to the cap."

Lyssa nodded. "The cap on a tower is much the same as the galleries on the wall tops?"

"Almost exactly the same," Brennar replied. "Both the towers and the walls are designed to work in the same way."

Lyssa nodded. They continued to climb.

They passed yet more doors off the stairway. Lyssa indicated one. "So all of this is storage?"

"Mostly," Brennar replied. "There are also rooms for the soldiers. In theory the whole of the tower garrison can live and sleep here during a siege, but it would be horribly cramped. When there is no immediate threat we live in barracks a short way away which are a lot more comfortable."

"And the tower is left unmanned?"

Brennar was shocked to momentary stillness by the absurdity of the idea. "Good Lord no!" he laughed. "Never. Not for a moment. Each tower garrison is divided into four shifts. Any given day three of these shifts are on duty for eight hours each, with the forth having a day off for relaxation and rest. Three days on, one day off, so the tower is always manned and ready to defend the city at any time of day or night."

"And should the dragons attack?"

"We have lookout posts in the mountains and on the city walls," Brennar said. "If they spot any significant numbers of dragons heading in our direction the alarm is sounded. The entire garrison heads for the tower. By the time the dragons arrive the tower is ready for them. The same is true for the other towers and the wall-top galleries."

"It all sounds very efficient and well considered."

"It is," Brennar assured her. "We have had a hundred years to get this right. We know our business when it comes to fighting dragons. Honestly, Lyssa, Tekmir is as safe as the mountains themselves. The dragons can't hurt us here. They've tried, God knows they've tried, but they've never come close to breaking us."

Lyssa was thoughtful. It was, indeed, looking remarkably well considered. "So how do you actually <u>fight</u> the dragons?"

"For that we need to climb to the cap," Brennar said, and lead the way.

The tower cap was a very different place. Firstly it was full of soldiers. Some relaxing and laughing, some playing cards and dice, some taking a nap, but many actively doing their duties as soldiers. Secondly there were great openings in the sides of the tower cap, windows out of which she could look over the city below.

Brennar explained. "The cap itself is made of steel, browned steel to prevent rust, though we regularly have to replace the odd panel that corrodes. The cap itself is on two floors, but each floor has shuttered firing positions like these." He indicated one of the open windows.

"But surely if dragons breathed at the cap the flame would come through and kill you all," Lyssa objected.

There was a general chuckle from the surrounding soldiers, a chuckle that suggested she had missed some important point.

"So you would think," Brennar said, "but watch this."

He took a lit torch from a sconce on the wall and approached one of the firing positions. There appeared to be a shutter above the opening, held open by a strut. He held the torch under the strut and, after a couple of seconds, the strut collapsed allowing the shutter to slam shut.

"Each firing position has a weighted cover to protect it," Brennar explained, "designed to shut under its own weight. The shutter is held open by the strut, but the strut itself is designed to fold and let the shutter close. What stops it doing so is one of these wax pegs." He returned the torch to the sconce and plucked from a small box what looked like a pale, translucent rod. "As soon as dragon breath hits it, it melts. The strut collapses, the shutter closes and the dragon fire remains outside. Yes, you get a short puff of flame before this happens, but the men at the firing positions wear goggles and dampened, canvas hoods to protect them from that. In truth it's mere moments before the position is closed, then the dragons can flame until they're blue in the face and do no harm at all."

He returned to the closed shutter, pushed it open, straightened the supporting strut and replaced the wax rod.

"Yet even with the shutters closed it must get burning hot in here, with dragons breathing on the outside of the cap?" Lyssa noted. "You're in a steel oven, and would get roasted like a joint of meat."

Brennar tapped the wall of the cap. "The cap has two skins," he said, "an inner and an outer, separated by about that." He held his hands about six inches apart. "Between the skins is an air gap with grills at the bottom and little chimneys at the top." He grinned. "Those are the other chimneys you noticed. As soon as the outer skin of the cap is heated by dragon fire the hot air rises, flowing up the chimneys and drawing in cold air at the bottom. This keeps the inner skin cool. Even with dragons breathing on the cap the inner wall gets barely too warm to place a hand on."

Damn, damn, damn, damn! For everything Lyssa said there seemed to be an answer. No wonder Bhuul and his battle dragons had tried and failed so often, these defences were rock solid. Dear God! She allowed herself one more try.

"Yet with the dragons flaming the outside of the cap the shutters will be closed," Lyssa murmured. "They can't hurt you, but you can't hurt them either."

Brennar beckoned her over to the open firing position and pointed. "See over there? That's Tower 6." He pointed in another direction. "And there is Tower 21. Both are within crossbow range. A little further out still ..." he pointed again "... is Tower 33. It's a bit far for a crossbow but but they can still reach us with a ballista ..."

"A ballista?"

Brennar chuckled. "I'll come to them later," he assured her. "The point is that even if a dragon manages to completely shut us down, he will <u>still</u> be ripped to pieces by the other, nearby towers. They protect us. We protect them. There is nowhere in this city where a dragon won't be attacked from at least two, and often three or four, directions. The galleries on the wall tops work the same way, with projecting bastions to ensure no dragon can attack without coming under intense attack themselves. It doesn't matter where they come from, by the time they're within ballista range we're hurting them, and by the time they're within crossbow range we're ripping them to pieces. Thankfully dragon fire is shorter than the range of a crossbow, so by the time they can flame us they're already suffering."

It was all horrifyingly efficient. "And a ballista?"

Brannar reached for a large, heavy cloth that was draped over something irregular. This he pulled aside to reveal something that looked like a massive crossbow mounted on a heavy, wooden trolley. "A ballista," he said. "Basically a very powerful spear thrower with long range. They throw those." He pointed to a rack on the wall, in which was stored a dozen heavy spears with long, steel points. "They'll easily reach eight hundred yards. Maybe twelve hundred at a pinch. Sure, they take an age to re-load, but they can hit a dragon

<u>long</u> before the dragon has any way of striking back. In a couple of attacks the dragons got so wary of our crossbows and ballistas that they stopped trying to attack us on foot at all, instead they flew overhead and dropped rocks."

"Didn't that do damage?"

"Sure," Brennar confirmed, "and killed many, but ultimately they can't destroy a city by throwing stones at it. If they want to destroy us they have to get their battle dragons on the ground and in our streets, flaming and smashing. That they just can't do without being wiped out."

Lyssa thought for a moment. "Thank you, Lieutenant of Guard," she murmured. "I think I now understand why this city has resisted dragon attack so long."

"And will resist it for a long time to come," Brennar grinned. "I hope you are reassured."

She nodded. "Oh yes."

She thanked Brennar for his attention and company and made her excuses. From the tower she made her way to a nearby shop where she purchased a map of Tekmir, a pen and some string. Back in her room at the inn she carefully marked the position of all the dragon towers and all the sections of wall-top gallery. She then used the string as a make-shift compass to draw arcs, representing the range of a heavy crossbow, around each.

When her work was done she looked at the result with a mixture of respect, understanding and horror. Brennar was right. There was not a single place in the city that was not in range of at least two points of attack. Every square foot was a death trap.

What in God's name could she do to break this city's defences? How could she give Bhuul and his battle dragons even a hint of a chance? She had to find something. <u>Had</u> to. She had promised

Thaakumek she would, but for the moment she couldn't think where to begin.

Leaving her map in her room she went again into the city. She didn't know what she was looking for, or even if she would recognise it when she saw it, but she needed something to trigger a new thought. Before arriving in Tekmir she had somehow believed that just seeing the Tekmiri defences from the inside would make her next step clear and obvious. The realisation that it was not that simple came as something of a shock.

She walked almost at random, and found herself in the very heart of the city. Here was a large market square filled with stalls and traders selling everything from food to fine jewellery. Among the traders milled a crowd. Not a vast crowd, the bitter cold ensured that, but a crowd still. To the west of the market square was a large, raised terrace accessible by six broad steps. Built on this terrace, but set back some way, was the municipal building of the city, the place from which Tekmir was governed. It was both elaborate in style and massive in size, set with several large, oaken doors and many windows decorated with fine carvings.

Attached to the front of the municipal building was a large awning of green and gold cloth, supported by wooden posts and stretched out by ropes, which sheltered almost the entire area of the terrace. Beneath the awning were rows of wooden tables and benches and, nearby, specially licensed vendors of food and drink who had been granted the right to sell their wares for consumption at those tables.

This winter's day was cold, but almost still. Without wind the coldness was of less concern to hardy mountain folk who knew how to wrap themselves properly against the chill. As a result the tables beneath the awning were still busy with folk of the city enjoying a leisurely meal or a drink to break the work of the day.

Lyssa made her way to the terrace and to one of the vendors. From this man she bought a large mug of 'klah', a heavy and slightly viscous hot beverage brewed from roasted nuts of the same name. She picked a small table and sat, gazing out over the market square.

She hadn't intended to listen to the conversations around her, indeed it had never occurred to her that she might hear anything of use or interest by pure chance, but as the minutes passed and savoured her drink she became aware of the sound of heated discussion from one of the nearby tables. Heated discussion in which one of the two voices was familiar to her. Her back straightened with realisation, and she began to actively eavesdrop.

"... listen, my friend," the unfamiliar voice urged, "I understand what you say, but ..."

"I doubt it!" The familiar voice cut him short. It was the man called Torm. The dragon expert she had met by her mother's corpse. "I doubt you have the slightest idea. Injustice remains injustice, Rann, no matter who the victim is."

"And yet there are many injustices," observed the man called Rann.

"And your point …?"

"My point," Rann's voice rose slightly in exasperation, "is that perhaps your priorities are not where they might best be! They've killed people, for God's sake, and you speak of injustice against them!"

Lyssa's back straightened a fraction further.

"Of course they've bloody killed people!" snapped Torm. "What choice do they have?"

"Not to," Rann answered emphatically.

61

"And what then? We invade their hunting grounds, we drive away their prey and they starve! For God's sake, Rann, do you really expect them <u>not</u> to fight for their lives? Wouldn't you?"

Rann sighed. "Listen, I understand … No! Don't interrupt, I really <u>do</u> understand, but this is not the time. Really it isn't. These last few weeks they've been attacking all over the place. Towns, villages, mines, wagon trains … everywhere. Humans are being killed, Torm. Your <u>own people</u>. There's just no sympathy for dragons in this city. Not now. Not when tales of dragon attack and human death are on every pair of lips."

"When, then?" snapped Torm. "It is not the time to speak of justice when the dragons are killing us, because our hearts are filled with hatred and fury. It is not the time to speak of justice when the dragons are <u>not</u> killing us, because to do so would decrease our mining profits! Peace or war makes no difference at all. It is <u>never</u> time to speak of justice for the dragons of the mountains. They have the bad luck not to be born human, and because of that misfortune we don't give a shit … ever!"

For twenty whole seconds there was silence.

"That is human nature, my friend." Rann's voice was soft. "You care for your own more than you care for those who are not your own. Yes, I don't want dragons to suffer and starve, but I am human and for me humans come first."

"And yet doesn't it occur to you," Torm asked, "that it might be better <u>for humans</u> not to make bitter enemies of dragons? Human beings are dead you say? Indeed they are, but why? Because we have made the dragons hate and fear us every bit as much as we hate and fear them. Probably more. It would be better for <u>both</u> peoples if we stopped killing each other, but for that we need give and take. Unfortunately we humans are very good at taking and damn poor at giving. Peace has to be earned and deserved."

"Or won," Rann murmured.

"Won?" Torm was horrified. "By what means, Rann? By the death of every dragon in the mountains? By the deliberate, systematic destruction of an entire race?"

"There are those who would claim the loss was worth the prize," Rann observed.

"And are you one of them?" Torm snapped. "That's monstrous!"

Lyssa cast a surreptitious glance in the direction of the two men. Torm, of course, she knew. The other man, Rann, was younger. He ran fingers through sand-coloured hair as Torm glared at him across the table they shared.

"No," Rann conceded, his voice soft. "I believe the wholesale slaughter of the dragon race would be, as you say, monstrous. Yet I have to admit that each time I hear of more killed, a village destroyed or a wagon train laid waste, I cannot help my heart hardening a little. It gets more … difficult … to remain just and reasonable."

Lyssa watched as Torm's anger faded. He ran fingers through his own, greying hair in almost perfect repetition of Rann just a few seconds before. "Forgive me, Rann. You are a good and fair man, and if I allowed myself to doubt that, even for a second, I was wrong to do so. I just find myself so frustrated that dragon kills human and human kills dragon. Two peoples at each others throats, each killing, when both would benefit so much from peace and understanding."

Rann snorted in disbelief. "There can be no peace and understanding between dragons and humans."

"There was before," Torm murmured.

"Bollocks!" Rann spat the obscenity. "Humans and dragons have been enemies for centuries."

"Indeed they have," Torm admitted, "but not for millenia. There was a time, long ago, when humans and dragons regarded each other with mutual respect. Perhaps not even then with great love and affection, but at least with the sort of understanding that meant they could speak as equals and avoid the insanity that overwhelms us these days."

Rann looked at him. "Then that was truly a golden time," he said, "but now long gone and never to return."

For thirty or forty seconds Torm sat in silence, considering Rann's words. When he spoke it was with infinite sadness. "Yes, my friend, I fear you may be right. Perhaps we have already passed that point at which there was any hope of turning back. The fear and mistrust may be too strong, too universal, too overwhelming in both peoples for peace to be an option now. When you get used to killing it becomes a habit, a habit harder to break with every corpse left defiling the ground. Perhaps too many have already died, both dragon and human, for hope to remain."

"And yet you still hope?"

Torm smiled. "I'm a fool," he said. "I shall hope until the day I die, however many are slain."

The conversation seemed to have run its course. After a few minutes of further pleasantries Rann took his leave and left. Lyssa remained watching Torm. For half and hour more he sat in thoughtful silence, then rose and turned ... seeing her as he did. He froze.

"Would you care to join me for a cup of klah, Mr Torm?" she called.

The spell of stillness was broken. A grin spread on Torm's lips and he stepped to her table. "I would be delighted," he said. "It will be the first time I have drunk klah with someone dead."

"Dead?"

"Some two weeks ago I received report that you had been eaten by a dragon, young lady."

"You, of all people," Lyssa observed, "should not have believed such a report."

"I didn't say I believed it," Torm corrected her, "merely that I had received it. Humans eaten and horses left? Your cloak conveniently burned with the pattern of your body, and the only other person gone a young woman of much the same height and build? Oh no. It sounded all too convenient, all too … staged ... to convince me."

"I told Bhuul that you would be the one to see through the deception, if any human did," Lyssa murmured.

"Bhuul?" Torm mused, gesturing Lyssa to silence so that he could try to answer his own question without prompting. "He's your queen's battle master, isn't he? A big, ugly brute of a dragon?"

Lyssa laughed. "Yes, he is," she confirmed, "and I suspect he might be flattered by your description, particularly as it fits him well." Torm sat while Lyssa collected two cups of klah and returned to him. "You mentioned to the other gentleman, Rann I believe he was called, the time when humankind and dragonkind lived in peace."

Torm flashed her a humorously stern look. "That tells me, young lady, that you were listening in on a conversation that was not of your concern."

"I do that," Lyssa admitted. "It's what spies do."

"So you're here as a spy, then?"

"Why else would I be here?" Lyssa asked.

Torm nodded slowly. "I guess that's true," he murmured. "I also guess your presence here does not bode well for the people of this city. Still, let us leave that for later. I did indeed mention to Rann a time of peace between your people and my own, but surely you know of this more than I do myself."

"Indeed I know," Lyssa murmured. "In fact I am, myself, a product of that time ..."

Torm nodded. "That I know."

"... What I didn't realise," Lyssa continued, "is that humankind still remembered. Your people are live shorter lives than mine, and by a large margin. You forget in a month what we remember for a decade."

"We have written records," Torm countered.

"Records which get left on the shelf to gather dust when what they say stops being convenient to hear," Lyssa noted, "but that is just human nature, I guess. Why concern yourself with a possibility of peace when the war is being won? Dragons are dying and the mountains are being stolen from them. Why should humans care any more?"

Torm took a deep breath. "They should, but perhaps they don't," he admitted. "So what would you have me say on the matter?"

"I'd like to know how you see that time, and what your records say of it."

Torm nodded. "Very well. Where should I begin?"

"At the beginning?" Lyssa suggested.

He looked at her a moment, then chuckled. "A good place to start," he said, "but sometimes it's hard to decide where the beginning truly begins. Perhaps we must go back some fifteen hundred years to a time rather similar to our own. In those days there were dragons in the mountains, much as now. Perhaps unlike now the humans lived almost exclusively in the lowlands, mainly farming and growing crops. Already there was trouble between the two peoples, but unlike these days it might have been the dragons who were the main aggressors. Hungry dragons, struggling to find food in mountains that were over-hunted, greedily eyed the humans' livestock. Farms were raided. Cattle, sheep, pigs, horses and other animals were consumed, and a great enmity built up between the peoples. Where the human farmers sought to protect their farms and animals they often ended up dying with them. In response the humans started trying to take the battle to the dragons with poisoned bait, spring-loaded barb traps and so on. Humans died. Dragons died. It was a bad time."

"Much like now indeed," Lyssa murmured.

"The big difference was that we had no mountain cities in those days," Torm continued. "We had not yet learned the art of defending ourselves against dragons, so in war against them we suffered and suffered badly. However in those days we had a single, great good fortune. Or, perhaps, two. The humans of this area were ruled by a man called Duke Petar Sagnan, and the dragons were ruled by a king named Dhuurchar."

"I know of Dhuurchar," Lyssa murmured. "His name is spoken among my people with the greatest respect. He is honoured as no other dragon. Yet I have heard far less of this man Petar Sagnan. What nature of man was he?"

"He was the Dhuurchar of the human race," Torm said. "Both rulers had wisdom, vision and understanding beyond that of their people as a whole. Dragons raged against humans, against their poisons and their spring traps that killed slowly and with terrible agony. Humans raged against thieving and murdering dragons that raided and attacked their farms. Each people could see with clarity the evil directed at them, but suffered from strange blindness when it came to the evil that they, themselves, inflicted."

"Truly like today!"

Torm nodded. "Yet Petar Sagnan and Dhuurchar could see both sides. Alone among their respective peoples they could see their own faults as well as those of the hated enemy. One day, when a dragon had been struck by a barb trap but not fatally injured, Petar Sagnan had the dragon released. The only condition was that the dragon would carry the duke's message to his king. This message asked for a meeting between the two rulers."

Lyssa chuckled. "Strangely our own recollection of events suggest the first approach was made by Dhuurchar."

Torm laughed. "Both memory and written record can be coloured by who writes, or who recalls," he observed. "Still, whoever arranged it, Dhuurchar flew out of the mountains to meet with the duke. They spoke long and deeply and each, in the other, recognised a noble and honourable soul. A brother, in effect. During that discussion each had the honesty to admit the failings of their own people. Each knew they could do nothing, personally, to end the injustice their people suffered, but each knew they could act to end the injustice their people inflicted. Dhuurchar returned to the mountains, the duke to his home, and both set about their work."

"The work was not easy," murmured Lyssa.

"Far from it," Torm agreed. "For either. Such hatred existed between the two peoples, such mistrust, that many believed the only solution was the wholesale extermination of the other. Rulers who demanded that human should not slay dragon, and that dragon should not slay human, were regarded by many as traitors to their own race."

"As would happen today," Lyssa observed, "if the rulers of today were to show similar vision."

Torm nodded. "Indeed they would, yet Petar Sagnan and Dhuurchar were not swayed by such nonsense. They were too noble for that. Their loyalty was given, not exclusively to their own people, but to the concept of justice itself. Neither was prepared to rule a people who butchered out of malice and hatred, so each turned their full efforts to ending the carnage. The duke banned the use of poisons and traps to kill dragons. Dhuurchar banned the raiding of human farms by hungry dragons. Each trusted the other to do what was right, while ensuring they did so themselves. The dragons gained an unexpected but mighty protector in the duke, and the human farmers were equally mightily protected by the dragon king. For sure there were lapses. Hungry dragons still occasionally found a cow or pig impossible to resist, and furious humans would still leave the occasional sheep in the open, laced with arsenic. Yet where this happened the ruler in question, human or dragon, sought out the criminal and administered proper and just punishment. In many ways it was hardest for the dragons because they were driven by overpopulation and genuine hunger, but in truth peace was to the benefit of both peoples."

Lyssa sighed. "Yet now, fifteen hundred years later, we are back where we were."

"Or even worse," Torm said. "During the lifetimes of the duke and the dragon king their understanding and mutual respect saved countless lives and much suffering, yet life is a temporary condition. The duke lived his seventy years and died. Dhuurchar, perhaps more tragically, was struck down by disease that left his body wasted and eventually took his life. After their deaths the ruler-ship of their peoples passed to others who were less wise and less noble. What was right shifted to what you could get away with on both sides. The ferocious mutual trust that Petar Sagnan and Dhuurchar had enjoyed was squandered in short-sighted pursuit of gain for one people at the expense of the other. All that was good was cast aside."

"And all that remained were the bi-forms," Lyssa murmured. "Which brings us to me."

Torm looked long and hard at her. "Indeed it does, young lady, and to a personal fascination of mine. During the later years of Duke Sagnan's and Dhuurchar's lives they became more than allies, they became friends. Yet friendship is difficult between dragon and human. The sheer difference in size, habitat and homeland makes it awkward. For this reason the duke approached a sorcerer of the time, a man named Losmar the Great. Great he truly was, far superior to the meagre conjurers we seem to have these days. Losmar devised a sorcery which would enable both human and dragon to assume the other's physical form, so they could visit the other in their own home and habitat. The duke and his immediate family were so enchanted, as was Dhuurchar and some of his relatives. Some ten humans and five dragons I believe. They were the bi-forms."

"Yet, curiously, the ability did not die with those it had been granted to," Lyssa murmured. "The off-spring of the bi-forms themselves became bi-forms, but the ability weakened with each generation. Dhuurchar could flash into human in an instant, and almost without thought. With later generations the change became more difficult, more agonising. Among the humans, where lives are short and the generations passed quickly, the bi-forms vanished long ago. Among the dragons I am the only one left, and I shall be the last. For me the change is almost beyond the limits of bearing. A searing, savage, burning pain."

"So are you descended from Dhuurchar himself?"

"No," Lyssa said, "but from his brother who was also enchanted. I am related to our current queen, but distantly."

Torm frowned. "The current queen is not a bi-form?" he asked.

"No," Lyssa replied. "Her father was, though he found the change as hard as I do myself. He only suffered it twice, once to human and then back to dragon, before declaring he never would again. Thaakumek, one further generation on, has lost the ability altogether."

"Yet while all else changes, the colour of the eyes never does," Torm murmured. "Duke Sagnan was a man of hazel eyes, and became a hazel-eyed dragon. Dhuurchar, as all dragons, had eyes the most brilliant, intense green. As a human his eyes remained that same colour."

"Which is how you recognised me for what I was when we first met," Lyssa said.

"To me it was obvious. Not to anyone else, but to me." Torm looked hard at her. "So what <u>are</u> you doing in Tekmir, dragon?"

"My duty to my queen, my people, and the memory of my mother who died, starved and shattered, on a bleak mountainside."

"Those sound like words of vengeance and butchery."

"Or the words of desperation and fear," Lyssa said. "We're dying, Torm, and unlike in Dhuurchar's day we have nothing to bargain for our lives with. Remember your friend Farron's words? We're not a threat, we're an inconvenience."

"Farron's ..." Torm paused, reconsidering his words. "... Farron's not a bad man. In fact he's a good man, honest and just. He's just ... short-sighted. He can see as far as his own people's suffering and welfare, but can see no further. Don't be too hard on him."

"On the contrary, I agree with him," Lyssa said. "We <u>are</u> just an inconvenience. We can't hurt you now that you have your mountain cities. Not really. We can destroy a few houses and wagon trains but nothing of note. We're beaten. In Petar Sagnan's time peace with the dragons was a great achievement, it avoided so much human suffering. What would peace with dragons buy you now? Nothing of great note, and it would lose you all the copper, tin, iron and other resources of the mountains. There can be no peace because, for you humans, it can never make sense. Yet we will not die quietly for the convenience of your people. We will die biting, clawing, flaming and bellowing our defiance. That way, when we're all gone, you will at least know you fought real dragons. You asked me why I am here? I am here looking for a way to destroy this city. I am looking for a weakness that will give Bhuul and his battle dragons a chance. I am looking for a way to be a little more than a mere inconvenience."

"Oh God," Torm murmured.

Lyssa sighed. "I'm sorry, my friend," she said, "but I have to do what is right for my people. I have to fight for them with every talent and strength I have, even when hope is so weak. I cannot just give up and watch my people die in despair."

"I understand." Torm's words were a whisper.

She looked at him. "And you, Torm, must do what is right for your <u>own</u> people. You must tell the city guard of me, and who I am, so that they can arrest me, interrogate me and slay me. That is <u>your</u> duty."

"But I can't!" Torm protested. "I just can't!"

"Then one or other of us," Lyssa murmured, "is doomed to betray our people. Either me by my failure, or you because your silence allowed my success."

Torm took a deep breath. "So be it." He stood. "And now, young lady, I think I shall return to my house. Today has been more challenging than I would have anticipated, and I suddenly have much to think about."

Lyssa stood and held out an arm. Torm grasped it. "If it's any consolation," she said, "you are, of all men I have spoken to, the one who appears truly just and fair. Of all men the most noble."

For a full minute he looked into her eyes before replying. "Remember that you, too, are noble," he whispered. Then he turned and walked away.

# Chapter Five

Back in her room at the inn Lyssa, once more, pulled out the map on which she had drawn arcs of crossbow range. Once more she examined it, then she screwed it up and hurled it on the flames burning in the room hearth. It darkened, crisped and flared.

"It doesn't matter," she muttered as she watched it burn, "how many times I look. The truth stubbornly refuses to become less true."

She had a problem. She had promised Thaakumek that Tekmir would fall. She had promised Bhuul that Tekmir would fall. She had promised her dead mother … no, not that Tekmir would fall, nothing as defined as that. Her mind had only become clear as she spoke to Thaakumek and heard her despair. Yet as she had stood, and wept, by her mother's head she <u>had</u> made a promise. A vague, unsure promise that somehow she would make things better. Three promises, the one to her mother burning most savagely in her heart. She <u>could not fail</u>.

Yet that was not her only problem. There was another, one that she barely acknowledged to herself. One she didn't <u>want</u> to acknowledge. Torm had spoken of peace, of a time when human and dragon respected each other and treated each other as equal. A golden time. Yet here she was, seeking a way to destroy a city and butcher sixty thousand people. Had she made the <u>right</u> promises?

"No, no, NO, <u>NO</u>!" she snarled to herself. "Khaajd, you fool! This is not the time to have silly doubts. You <u>know</u> what you have to do. You just have to find the way to damn well <u>do it</u>!"

Yet how? What was the next step? She found herself at a loss.

"Food," she murmured. "You cannot think when your stomach is complaining."

She made her way to the common room, and there ordered a meal and mead to drink with it. She ate, she drank, she sat, she thought … and inspiration failed to materialise.

In the absence of inspiration, resort to blind and stubborn hope. The Tekmiri guardsmen may be efficient and disciplined in normal duties, but they had not seen any real trouble with dragons for over two decades. Perhaps their discipline and order would crumble under pressure. Lyssa resolved to stir them up and see what happened. It was now about three in the afternoon, and once more she headed out in to the streets of Tekmir. This time she was looking for somewhere specific, a vantage point from which she could get a good view of the surrounding mountains. Thankfully she had seen such a place while at the market square. A tower. Not one of the dragon towers but an ornament built for decoration and covered in statues, what was more important were the public stairs within which lead up to a railed viewing balcony at the top.

She climbed the stares and stood at the rail high above the market square, scanning the surrounding skyline. There, to the north east and about ten miles distant, was a dragon on a mountain top. He did not attempt to conceal himself, but instead perched in full view gazing balefully at the city with brilliant, burning green eyes. It was not Bhuul but another battle dragon almost his match in weight. The dragons watched the humans and the humans watched the dragons, both with ill will in their hearts.

She now went to the same shop where she had earlier bought a map of the city. Here she bought a second map, not of the city but of the surrounding lands. Back in her room at the inn she marked where she had seen the dragon and examined the surrounding area closely. The mountain on which the dragon perched had an abandoned copper mine at the bottom, probably abandoned <u>because</u> of the dragon on the peak. That was convenient, because it meant there was a rough road leading almost all the way there.

So getting to the dragon wouldn't be a problem. Getting there unseen might be more difficult. Brennar had mentioned there were lookouts in the mountains. He called them 'lookout posts', but for sure they would not be permanent structures or Bhuul would have destroyed them. Patrols, then. Men working their way through the mountains, keeping their eyes open and themselves concealed, never in the same place twice. The last thing she needed was a patrol seeing her close to, or worse still talking to, a dragon.

The next morning she informed the innkeeper she would be away for a few of days and paid him in advance to reserve her room. She dressed in warm, travel clothing, packed a tent and food for four days, mounted her horse and headed for the city gate. At the gate she was, of course, challenged by the city guardsmen who were concerned to see a solitary woman riding out of the city unprotected. She decided the best policy was was to tell almost the truth.

"I saw a dragon to the north east yesterday," she declared.

"You'll <u>always</u> see a dragon to the north east," came the gate guard's reply. "That's where they watch us from. There's three of them that take turns. A really big, evil looking bastard ..." That would be Bhuul. "... and a couple of others who are not much smaller and no easier on the eye. So what of these dragons, miss?"

"I thought I'd ride a bit closer so that I could get a better look," she said. "You can't really see a dragon properly at ten miles, despite their size."

The man looked at her as if she was completely mad. "You're going to ride a horse up to a dragon?" he asked. "You know what that makes you?"

"A fool?" she suggested sweetly.

"A self-delivery dragon snack," the guard replied. "Human appetiser and horse main course."

Lyssa laughed. "I don't intend to get <u>that</u> close," she assured him.

"If the dragon spots you," he warned, "how close you get will be his decision, not yours."

"Then I'd better not be spotted."

"You will be," the man warned her. "Dragons have eyes like gimlets. He'll see you before you get within five miles. Honestly, miss, it's not worth the risk just to see a dragon close up. Content yourself with the view from here and enjoy the distance."

She leaned forward to whisper in conspiratorial fashion. "But where's the sense of adventure in that?" she asked. "Come on! Taking a few risks is what adds spice to life. If you do only what is safe you may live seventy years, but you'll find every one a tedium."

He looked at her. "Well," he admitted, "I have no authority to stop you, miss. We are gate guards here, not jailers. If you wish to ride into the mountains to go dragon watching then that is your choice and your risk to take, all I can do is warn you against it."

"I hear your warning and thank you for it, soldier," she said. "But, being a stubborn and difficult girl at heart, I shall choose to ignore it and take my chance in the mountains."

"Then I hope we meet again so that I can buy you a mead in celebration of your continued life," the guardsman said, and waved her through the gate.

The ride proved tediously uneventful. The mountains were barren. No human brigands or bandits lurked here, close to the city and overlooked by a dragon. No cougars stalked. The occasional hyrax scuttled, and a single eagle flew overhead, but other than that the wilderness through which she rode was almost devoid of interest.

Following her newly bought map she headed towards where she had spotted the dragon the day before, but due to the winding mature of mountain roads and paths a straight line distance of ten miles would take a long day by horseback. It would be getting dark when she made her final approach to the dragon. Dark enough to avoid the prying eyes of patrols.

She muttered a silent word of hope that the dragon had good eyes, and that Bhuul had remembered to warn him she might be making contact. If he had not their meeting would be very short, very hot and extremely unsatisfactory. Still, that was for the future. For the moment she could enjoy a leisurely ride along mountain paths and tracks, breathing air free from the smells of humanity.

As night began to fall she was, she estimated, three miles from where the dragon watched. She made camp. She fed, watered and tethered her horse. She lit a fire and cooked a meal. She pitched a tent. She did everything a watching Tekmiri patrol would expect her to do, and in the gathering gloom, retired to the her tent with much show of yawning, stretching and apparent weariness. Then an hour later, when it was darker by far and her fire had burned to embers, she emerged dressed in her darkest clothes and headed up the track.

It was a surprisingly long and hard climb. The track was rough and stony, with many an obstacle to trip over if she was unwary. The last thing she wanted was to be disabled in the mountains by sprained or broken ankle, but she dared not use a lamp for fear of being seen. Thankfully the sky was not entirely dark. A more-than-half moon gleamed, leaving the mountains around her lit a dull grey. Looking forwards and up to the skyline she couldn't see the dragon at all. Damnation. You'd think a battle dragon would be big enough to see, even at night.

By an hour before midnight she had reached the wreckage of the abandoned mine, and the end of the path. Still there was no dragon to be seen against the grey of the sky. She looked around her and softly called. "I don't know where in the name of hell you're hiding," she said, "but if you can hear me, show yourself!"

<u>Then</u> the saw him! A great arch of neck rose from the dark of the mountain top against the marginally less dark sky beyond. "Hiding?" The voice was the rumble of dragon speak. "I have just been lying here peacefully, enjoying the cool of the night, and watching you approach."

"You could at least have let me know," Lyssa grumbled.

"How?" he asked. "Call to you so that every human within a mile would hear?"

It was a fair point. Dragon voices were powerful and carried for miles. Now that she was close to him the dragon was making strenuous efforts to keep his voice quiet. Practically whispering.

"I am Khaajd," Lyssa said.

"I assumed you were," the dragon replied, "which is to your good. Had I not, both you and your horse would already be eaten. I am Mhiirak, a battle dragon and colleague of Bhuul."

Lyssa had not met Mhiirak before, but that hardly mattered. Any dragon Bhuul chose to watch over Tekmir would be well chosen. She nodded an acknowledgement and greeting. "I need to get a message to Bhuul. I am investigating the defences of the city below, but I need to see how they react to an emergency. I'd like Bhuul to do something to stir them up. To frighten them a little."

Mhiirak remained silent for at least twenty seconds. "You want an attack on the city?"

"Good God, no!" Lyssa replied. "Dragons would die. That's the last thing I want, just something to make them worried. Something to make them think that this day is different from all the previous days and they have to be prepared."

Mhiirak considered. "That should be no problem," he mused. "I'm sure if a wing of battle dragons hove into view, overflew the city, and dropped a few rocks then the humans would take proper note."

Battle dragons had a rather limited structure as a fighting force, but they had two distinct sizes of group that worked together. A 'flight' was twelve dragons. A 'wing' was five flights, sixty dragons. The total number of the battle dragons was between six and seven wings, so certainly almost a sixth of the queen's full strength flying overhead and bombarding Tekmir with rocks would be taken seriously indeed!

"Of course I'd rather not have a rock dropped on my head," Lyssa murmured.

"If you're in the city at the time you must take your chance like anyone else," Mhiirak replied. "We will be flying high, above their missile weapons, and will not be able to see and avoid individual humans."

A fair point. "You could, of course, overfly the city and not drop rocks?" Lyssa suggested.

Even in the dim light she saw him tongue wrap. "You are suggesting we fly over the crawling vermin in their nest and do nothing? Oh please, Khaajd! We're battle dragons!"

Lyssa sighed. "Alright, Mhiirak," she conceded. "I take the point. Drop your rocks and I shall just have to hope I'm not under one."

Mhiirak's massive head turned to her, his green eyes pierced the night-time darkness. "So when do you want this to happen?"

"At dawn," she replied. "Not before four days from now. That way I can be back in the city and settled. I don't want anyone to connect what happens with my visit to the mountains. Yet within a week. Do you think that can be done?"

Mhiirak mused. "I don't see why not," he rumbled. "You are the queen's favourite, so what Khaajd wants Khaajd will get. Besides, I doubt there will be any reluctance on Bhuul's part to lob a few rocks at the city. I can imagine him being rather enthusiastic about the idea."

"Excellent," Lyssa said. "I shall make sure I'm somewhere I can watch the results each dawn until it happens."

"And if, for any reason, we cannot do it I will personally put up signal flame," Mhiirak replied. "Is there any particular time of day to do so, that you would have the best chance of seeing it?"

"Just do it at night," Lyssa said, "and make it obvious. Trust me, signal flame in the mountains will be seen by the guard on watch, and news will spread through the city. I will hear of it even if I don't see it myself."

So, arrangements complete, she made her farewells and headed back down the path to her camp and horse. Once there she was able to snatch barely an hour's sleep before rising, making a pretence of being well rested, and heading back to the city.

By the time she arrived at the Dragon's Fall inn it was late evening and she was exhausted. Two full days in the saddle and the night between scrambling along mountain paths had left her utterly drained. She took her horse to the inn stables, left instructions for his care, and headed for the main inn door. In her tiredness she misjudged her step, tripped and fell in an ungainly heap on the cobblestones.

An arm looped under her own. "Up you get, deary!" The voice cracked with a mixture of age and humour. "It's not right for you young ones to fall and us oldies to help you up. Should be the other way."

Lyssa clambered back to her feet and found herself looking into a smiling, wrinkled face crowned with stone-grey hair. "Thank you, madam," she murmured.

The woman saw the dullness of eye and heard the dullness of voice. The smile dropped, replaced by concern. "Are you alright, dear?"

"Yes," Lyssa said. "Yes, alright. Just tired. Too much work and too little sleep."

"Then you must go straight home and to your bed!" she was commanded.

Home? Home was a cave in the mountains a thousand miles away. "I … I have a room here, at the Dragon's Fall."

"Then inside and straight to sleep with you," the woman chided, leading her to the inn door and opening it for her.

Lyssa stepped through the door and then turned back, but by now the elderly woman had already turned and was making her slow way along the street. "Thank you," she murmured, unheard, to the retreating back. Then a soft whisper to herself. "Thank you for help and concern. I shall try and repay your kindness by killing you and all you love." She made her way to her room and slept.

Lyssa didn't know when Bhuul would stir up the defences for her, so she started rising early and heading out into the streets before dawn so she would be positioned to see the action whenever it happened. It happened on dawn of the fifth day.

The first sign that this particular morning would be different from all the others was the ringing of bells. They started ringing out on the top of the eastern city wall, but almost before she had been able to register the sound it was answered. As fast as the noise itself could carry the alarm was carried with it. Each wall top gallery and tower cap heard and added their own bell to the growing clamour. In thirty seconds at most bells clanged throughout the city. Yet that was not the only sound.

Lyssa had positioned herself in a quiet and shadow-filled hiding place between a dragon tower and its associated barrack hall. From within the guard's hall came voices. Barked orders. The clattering of metal and the pounding of feet. Within a few seconds the first few soldiers appeared, clothing awry, sword belts in their hands and their mail flung, for now, over their shoulders, running for the tower. Within another thirty seconds the few had become many. Men throwing away the bread and klah of breakfast. Men dressed for their beds, but with clothes and equipment in their arms. Men half washed. Half shaved. All scrambling to the tower. Down the streets came others, obviously those who were off duty but still heard the bells and snatched up their equipment to join their brothers in the tower. Dozens of men.

Lyssa, from her previous visit to Tower 17, had a good idea of what the standard strength was. Within five minutes of the alarm being raised this had doubled, and still more men ran. Admittedly the extra soldiers had rushed to the tower unprepared, but Lyssa had no doubts that once inside the armour would be donned, the helmets would be placed on heads and the sword belts would be buckled. Within scant minutes these extra men would be in position, adding to the strength of the tower's defence. It was not pretty, by any means, but it looked worryingly effective. Long before the first dragon appeared in the sky overhead she looked up at the tower top and saw the firing positions so full of faces there was barely space for more.

Then came the dragons, flying high. Five great V shapes, painted against the sky, each of twelve dragons. They flew too high for crossbows to reach them. Even the odd ballista spear that arched upwards fell short. Above the ringing of the bells she could hear the roar of distant wings. Then specks fell from the dragons. Tiny specks, so high, but growing rapidly. Falling rocks the size of horse hammered down on shop and square, on tower and inn, on road and traveller. Lyssa heard the crashes, the screams. The shattering of wood and tile.

Then, almost as soon as it had begun, it was over. The dragons wheeled away to the north and disappeared, leaving a city in shock. All had changed in those few minutes. Tekmir had not come under dragon attack for more than two decades and the people had begun to believe the dragons had given up on them. That they were truly in a place safe from the old enemy. Even when dragons attacked the nearby wagon trains and towns the people of Tekmir had not seen it as their problem. Tragic and unfortunate, for sure, but distant.

In truth each dragon had only carried two rocks, one in each fore claw. Tekmir had been hit by one hundred and twenty stones, killing a dozen and causing some damage. It was not a great event by any meaningful measure, but it shattered the cosy illusion of immunity. It was in those few minutes that the people of Tekmir realised they were very much at war. As Lyssa walked back to the inn she saw the people of the city walking the streets and looking at the damage, and for the first time there was fear in their eyes.

Yet in Lyssa's own heart she could see no reason for them to be fearful. She had hoped that, somehow, the dragons would appear and then the soldiers would react. That there would be a lag in which the dragons could attack before the defences were at their maximum strength. This little experiment had demonstrated nothing of the kind. Tekmiri patrols in the mountains had seen the approaching dragons and sent warning. The warning had spread and the soldiers had been ready, in position, before the dragons could even get there. There would be no attacking <u>this</u> city by surprise.

What the hell could she do to give Bhuul a chance against this place?

At her room she took of the dark clothing she wore to skulk unseen in the city streets and dressed in less sinister looking clothing, suitable to be seen in. Heading out into the city she made her way to the market square for breakfast, a mug of klah and a long think. An hour, a breakfast, and three mugs of klah later she was still sitting there, but nothing by way of inspiration had struck.

"Young lady?"

Her back straightened at the familiar voice. "Mr Torm?"

"May I join you?"

She gestured to the other bench at the table. He sat. For a minute they looked at each other. Her eyes green, his troubled.

"It's been a long time since we last had trouble with dragons," he observed, "and yet today we had a wing of them bombarding the city with rocks. Some dozen dead, I hear, with many more hurt. Buildings smashed, roads broken and the people of the city feeling less safe in their homes and beds."

"Indeed." Her voice was flat.

"Was this your doing ..." he leaned forwards to whisper "... <u>Khaajd</u>?"

"A few rocks won't make this city fall."

"Indeed they won't," Torm replied, "but that was not the question I asked. Are you, personally, responsible for the death of twelve people?"

She took a deep breath. "I didn't drop a single rock."

Torm's eyes narrowed. "You do not need to drop a rock to be responsible for their dropping."

"True," she admitted. "Then I shall be honest. I wished to see how the soldiers would react to an alarm of dragon attack. For that I needed an alarm for them to react to. I contacted Bhuul and asked him to arrange such an alarm. This fall of rocks was the result."

He nodded. "Then you have the deaths of a dozen people on your conscience, as do I for not alerting the city guard to who you were the moment I knew."

"This is <u>war</u> Torm. People die in war. It's the nature of the beast."

"Yet what have those twelve people done to you, that they deserve to die?"

"They have stolen what is ours!" Lyssa roared.

Around them heads turned at the sound of angry words, but not knowing the context in which they were said learned little from the glance.

Torm looked around him. "We cannot speak here," he muttered. "We could be overheard. Come with me, Khaajd. My house is nearby. There we can talk in private."

He lead her through the city streets until he reached a door. Taking a key from his belt pouch he opened it and invited her in. Inside was a shrine to dragonkind. Paintings of dragons adorned the walls. Statues of dragons stood in room corners. Dragon teeth acted as paperweights, holding down parchment on his writing desk. Everywhere there were books, every written word that a man could find about her people gathered in one place. He showed her to a chair and sank into one himself. He waited for her to speak.

"Where this city stands dragons once lived," she murmured. "Where this city stands once roamed goats and other prey for dragons to eat. My people are having their homeland stolen by your people and you ask where the harm is? Is watching your young starving not enough?"

"There are many mountains."

"Which means we should not care if a few are taken from us?" Lyssa asked. "Then a few more, and a few more, until one day we wake up and realize that we have nothing left and all is gone? Tekmir is not the only city in dragon lands. Then there are the roads, the villages, the towns, the mines! We are losing <u>everything</u> Torm. Everything. I admit we're losing it slowly and we have a great deal yet to lose, but it's all going. City by city, road by road, mine by mine our <u>lives</u> are being stolen from us. Do you expect us not to fight? Do you expect <u>me</u> not to fight? My problem is not the dozen people I have killed in Tekmir this morning, but the <u>sixty thousand</u> who are yet to kill!"

Torm ran his hands through his hair. "So that really is it? You want to kill <u>everyone</u>? Women and children? Old and young?"

"I want the place now known as the city of Tekmir returned in full to its rightful owners, the dragons," she said, "and that means returned to what it was, empty ground. Every building gone. Every road gone. Every street and inn and shop gone. Every <u>human</u> gone. Nothing left. I want mountain goats walking where we now sit."

"And the people?"

"I have no ill will towards humans," Lyssa said. "In fact I find human company agreeable. Some humans I like a great deal. I don't want you to suffer, I just don't want you <u>here</u>. Go to your own homes, your own lands, and leave the dragons alone."

"But you cannot expect sixty thousand people to leave."

"No," Lyssa said. "They will not leave. That's why they have to die."

"But Khaajd! This is no more right than what we are doing to you! Yes, I admit our crimes. On behalf of the whole of humankind I admit them, but wholesale slaughter of a city is not the way. Surely there must be some possibility of compromise between our peoples?"

"What does 'compromise' mean, Torm?" Lyssa asked. "Does it mean that what's already stolen from us must remain stolen? That hunting grounds already lost remain lost? Human thieves can take what they want and the dragons must 'compromise' by not asking for it back? Will you humans be gracious enough to allow us to live in an ever shrinking homeland, in ever shrinking numbers, starving and beset on all sides, until we're so weak that you don't need our 'compromise' any more? Until you can butcher the last few of us and have done? No, Torm! We will <u>not</u> 'compromise'. We will fight. We may die, we may <u>all</u> die, but we will take as many of you to the grave with us as we can."

Torm eyes closed. His head dipped. "That's the way you really see it?" he asked. "A final fight to the death, a war of utter annihilation?"

"How else can it be?" Lyssa asked. "When we spoke last we told a pretty tale of peace. Of Dhuurchar and Petar Sagnan and understanding between our two peoples, yet what happened in the end? Both peoples stopped believing in justice and started seeking all they could. Don't misunderstand me, Torm. I know this is just as much a dragon failing as a human one, and that we are as likely to be dishonest as you, but the end is the same. Peace and decency fails, and self interest runs riot. We had Duke Petar Sagnan and Dhuurchar, king of dragons. For a brief moment two great rulers, towering giants among humans and dragons alike, managed to hold back the tide of selfish dishonesty and dishonour. Yet once they were gone ..." Her voice faded to nothing.

"Once they were gone the peace they founded fell apart," Torm whispered. "The inherent dishonesty and self-interest of both peoples overwhelmed their sense of justice. Promises were broken on both sides and the butchery resumed."

"We just returned to being what we really are," Lyssa murmured.

"And you really see no hope of a return to peace?"

"Do you?" asked Lyssa. "Look around you, Torm. This is Tekmir. How long has this city stood here?"

Torm considered. "It's difficult to say when Tekmir truly started being a city," he replied, "but it was certainly one fifty years ago, and with equal certainty not one fifty years before that."

"So somewhere between fifty and a hundred years," Lyssa said. "Humans live about seventy years."

Torm nodded. "About that."

"And most of the people of this city are well under fifty," Lyssa observed. "These people have never known a world without Tekmir. It's 'always' been here, for them at least. It's theirs. They know it in their heart. Their home. Where they have lived all their lives."

Torm nodded. "And yet dragons live far longer."

"Indeed they do," Lyssa confirmed. "A dragon lives twelve hundred years. I'm a young dragon, really young, yet even I have lived three hundred and fifty! There's hardly a dragon alive, certainly not an adult, who doesn't remember the world before Tekmir. For us this city is new and monstrous. We all remember when this place was utterly ours, and we are as sure it's ours as any man or woman living within these walls is sure it's theirs. How can there be understanding between two peoples who both <u>know</u> they're right, and that justice is on their side? There is no common ground. None at all."

"So all that's left is to fight to the death?"

"If you can suggest an alternative, then I would be most grateful to hear it," Lyssa said, "but I can think of none. Maybe, just possibly, if we had a new Petar Sagnan and a new Dhuurchar we could turn aside the course of this war, but do you see them?"

Torm thought. "The current duke is a good and just man," he said, "but there is a world of difference between being a good and just man, and having the extraordinary gifts, courage and strength of purpose that set Petar Sagnan apart from others."

"And our queen, Thaakumek, is ferociously passionate about her people," Lyssa said. "She is courageous, strong and filled with fire in her soul. I have no doubts <u>at all</u> that she would cast aside her own life in a moment if she believed doing so would save her people. She is noble and proud in the extreme, but is she another Dhuurchar? <u>Can</u> there be another Dhuurchar? If I'm being honest I cannot believe."

Torm nodded in resignation. "So what now?"

"Now," Lyssa said, "I continue to do what I am here to do, not that I have any idea how to do it. You have to decide your own course. If you decide I must be arrested by your city guards then I can hardly fault that decision, it's probably what I would do in your place. If you do I go by the name of Lyssa Urdak, and I currently stay at the Dragon's Fall inn in Temple Square. They can find me there."

He looked at her. "You may be a dragon, and an enemy of my people, but you're damn honest about it."

"And you may be a human that is about to have me arrested, interrogated and slain," she replied. "But at least I know that whatever you do, it will be done in the firm belief that it's right."

"Arse!" he swore. "I <u>have</u> no 'firm beliefs', only doubts and questions. No idea at all what's right and wrong."

"Life is so much simpler when you don't care, isn't it?" Lyssa observed.

# Chapter Six

Lyssa headed back to the inn to think and found the common room, for the first time since she had arrived there, almost deserted. Dragons flying overhead and rocks being dropped on people had changed the mood here as well. Most who would have been spending a day of leisure in jovial company, with a mead in their hands, had other matters on their mind. The few who were there drunk in sombre silence. Lyssa ordered a meal and mead for herself.

"It's a sad day," the innkeeper murmured as he poured her glass. I'd thought we'd got past all this. I thought they'd learned to leave us alone." 'They', of course, needed no further definition.

"They've barely started," Lyssa murmured in reply.

He looked at her. "You think so?"

"You believe they'll just drop a few rocks and disappear?" She returned his glance. "After more than twenty years not touching Tekmir you think today's ... nonsense ... is all they've got? No. This is just a small opening ploy. An appetiser. The main course is yet to come."

"But what can they do?" The man's voice rang with a strange mixture of bravado and fear. "We have the towers and the walls. We have the soldiers. They <u>know</u> they can't beat us."

"I have no idea," Lyssa almost whispered, and in truth she did not.

The innkeeper glanced over her shoulder and grumbled. A good natured grumble, for sure, but still a grumble. "Soth you bastard!" he called to someone behind her. "Do you really have to drink here? Every time you do it takes us a week to quell the rumours."

Lyssa turned to look. Soth was a large, jovial looking man who managed to grin despite the gloom of the day. He shrugged his shoulders and called back. "A man's got to drink somewhere, and you have fine ale."

Lyssa looked back to the innkeeper. He winked at her. "The local rat-catcher," he explained with a chuckle. "A good man and excellent company, but if ever a rat-catcher walks into an inn ..."

"... people will assume he's here on business." Lyssa completed the thought.

Soth joined them at the bar, buying a mug of strong ale. "So who's the cute girl?" he asked the innkeeper, grinning and nodding towards Lyssa. "Too good for you, my friend. You need to stick to your normal type."

"A guest," the innkeeper replied, "and one I'd rather you didn't annoy."

Soth turned to Lyssa. "If I'm annoying you, say so lass," he declared. "Then I'll bugger off and annoy some other sod instead."

Lyssa laughed. "And allow someone else to enjoy <u>my</u> annoyance? Not a bit of it, Mr Soth." She held out a hand. "I'm Lyssa Urdak, staying here for a few days. I understand you're a rat-catcher."

Soth chuckled. "Much to the distress of our friend the innkeeper here. He curses every time I come and give him my business, ungrateful bastard!"

Lyssa looked back to the innkeeper. "Tell you what," she said. "If you'll have my food sent to that table over there ..." she indicated "... then Mr Soth can join me and tell me all about rats."

The innkeeper raised an eyebrow. "And a delightful conversation that will be, miss," he grinned.

Lyssa lead Soth to the table and they sat. "So what brings you to an inn and this hour of the morning?" she asked, sipping her mead.

Soth's joviality faded a moment. "When the sky is full of dragons," he replied, "I thought I would rather be here drinking ale than sat alone in my home thinking. You can have too much time to think."

Lyssa nodded. "I couldn't agree more," she said. "So let's change the subject. Tell me of rats."

Soth's grin returned. "Now why would a pretty girl like you want to talk of rats?" he asked. "I'd have thought you would be more interested in fine dresses and the latest styles of wearing your hair."

"Because they're smaller than dragons?" Lyssa suggested.

Soth considered the point. "Fair enough," he said. "I'll buy that."

"Have you been a rat-catcher for long?"

"All my life," Soth said. "I've always liked rats. Had 'em as pets when I was a nipper. They're bright little beasts. Real survivors."

"And yet now you catch them," Lyssa observed. "Doesn't that bother you?"

"Hmm. 'Catch' is a euphemism, miss. I kill 'em and, yes, it's a bit sad. I admit that, but it's got to be done. A rat's a fine little creature and, if it lived where it should, I'd wish it well. But you cant have 'em in your cellar, crapping on your floor and eating your victuals. It's not the rat that's the problem. It's where the rat is that's the problem, if you get my drift."

"Oh yes." Lyssa most certainly got the drift of that. "Yet when they're in the wrong place they must be difficult to deal with."

Soth nodded. "If there's just a few of 'em then you can trap 'em," he said. "I set big, heavy snap traps with a bit of bait on the trigger. Along comes the rat, snap and that's the end of the story. Broken back. It's when things have got way out of hand that it gets harder. When you're not talking about a dozen or so, but a couple of hundred. Then you have to turn to other methods that are a lot nastier."

Lyssa found herself tensing. "When you have a wholesale infestation?"

"Yes indeed. Then there's little option but to turn to poison. I don't like it, miss, if truth be told. It's a nasty, slow way for a rat to die. They really don't deserve that, poor little buggers. They're just trying to live their lives after all."

Lyssa nodded slowly. "Poison? Yes ..." she found herself murmuring "... I guess that might do it, but you're right. It is a nasty way to kill things. Even vermin."

Soth caught the changed tone in her voice. He looked at her. "You alright, miss?"

She brought her mind back to the moment. "Yes, Soth. I'm sorry. My mind slipped away to somewhere it shouldn't. I must confess I'd thought talking of rats would be more comforting than talking of dragons, but now I'm not so sure."

"I didn't want to upset you, miss."

Lyssa forced a laugh. "No upset caused," she assured him, "but maybe a change of subject is in order. What else interests you beside rats?"

And so the subject changed, and ranged in many ways as Lyssa's meal arrived and she ate. Yet wherever the words lead there was always that haunting thought that wouldn't go away. The thought of rats ... and poison.

With her meal eaten she took her leave of Soth and headed into the city streets. She needed to walk, and think. This was all suddenly very different. Before she had doubts, but the very fact that she did not know how to destroy Tekmir meant she could ignore them. They were something to be faced later, to be addressed later, when the method had been found.

But now ... Dear God! Now the method had been found. Poison. A weapon with which one can kill thousands. Now there was no ignoring the doubts. Now they were real and immediate. Now she had to make the decision, whether she really could and should do this.

"A human's a fine little creature," she murmured the paraphrased words to the street ahead, "and, if it lived where it should, I'd wish it well. But you cant have 'em in your mountains, pumping filth into your lakes and scaring off your victuals. It's not the human that's the problem. It's where the human is that's the problem."

But she had not met a single human being that she actually wanted to kill, not one, and humans that she actively did not want to kill were everywhere. Torm. The innkeeper. Soth. The old lady who had helped her to her feet. The streets were full of them.

Yet how could she not? On an intellectual level it was obvious. She knew of the humans' ongoing encroachment into the dragons' mountains, and that the dragon specific defences of Tekmir and the other mountain cities made this encroachment irresistible. She knew the humans would have no reason to stop taking her people's home, because the cities meant they could do so without meaningful risk. She knew that her people were doomed. Absolutely. Utterly. Completely. And that their only hope was to break the human cities. The humans <u>had</u> to learn to fear dragons again or they would all die.

Yet to personally, physically buy lethal poison and use it to unleash agonizing, slow death on thousands of people? That was a different matter. There was nothing intellectual about that. It was vicious, savage, brutal mass murder of the innocent, and even a dragon's blood can run cold at such thoughts.

"Who do you love more, Khaajd?" she whispered to herself. "Dragons or humans?"

That, finally, is what it came down to. Was she a dragon who fought to save her own people, or had she now become a human, casting aside the loyalties of her blood?

She walked the streets, alone despite the crowd around her. She wrestled with that one question. She hoped that clarity would somehow appear and that the decision would be made for her, yet clarity did not appear and the decision resolutely refused to be made … unless she made it herself. From moments like this there is no escape. No flight to the comfort of procrastination. She had to grit her teeth and choose where she stood.

There was only one choice. She stood with the dragons.

She could no longer afford doubts. She could no longer afford compassion. Humans were rats, rats in a cellar. They had to go. They had to be poisoned. They had to die. There was no other option. Suddenly the Lyssa who looked upon the streets of Tekmir was a very different creature. A cold-eyed, ruthless, vicious Lyssa who had wrestled long and hard with her inner kindness and then hurled it aside.

Something blue dropped past her face and fell at her feet.

"Sorry!" came a call.

Lyssa looked for the voice. Above her, on the upper floor balcony of a house, sat a young woman with an apologetic face. On her lap a child, his eyes just beginning to brim with tears. "He's dropped Mr Dog," the mother explained.

Lyssa looked down, stooped and picked up the object that had fallen at her feet. It was a knitted, stuffed child's toy, though she wouldn't have recognised it as a dog without being told. Certainly not as it was blue. She looked back at mother and child. The child's eyes widened and he reached out a hand towards her.

"He loves him," the woman explained. "Wait a moment, I'll bring him down."

For twenty seconds Lyssa waited until the door of the house opened and the woman stepped out, child in arms. Lyssa held out Mr dog and the child reached, and grasped, and instantly put the knitted animal's rear leg in his mouth. The look of joy and relief on his face was a wonder to behold.

"Thank you," the mother said, and then turned to her son. "Say thank you to the pretty lady."

"Ankoo."

"That's the best he can do at the moment," the mother said.

Lyssa paused a few seconds. "And much appreciated," she murmured.

The woman dropped her son onto her hip and turned back into her house, Mr Dog hanging by a leg from the child's hand. The door closed. Damn! That could hardly have come at a harder moment. If only this city could be filled with soldiers and crossbows she could kill them all, perhaps not with joy but at least without deep regret. Yet to plot the death of a mother who loved her child, and a child who loved his blue, knitted dog? That hurt. That <u>really</u> hurt.

She had to get out of the city. She had to get out of it <u>now</u>, before anything else happened and her resolve crumbled. She headed back to the inn and up the stairs to her room, ignoring the innkeeper who seemed to want to attract her attention. In her room she stooped over her travel bags, pushing her belongings in.

There was a knock at the door. She paused. "Come in."

It was the innkeeper. "I'm sorry, miss, but I saw you come back. Are you alright? After you left earlier Soth was worried that he might have upset you. He said you seemed ... well ... <u>changed</u> after your conversation."

"Please reassure Mr Soth that any problems I may have had resided entirely in the six inches between my own ears," Lyssa replied. "Neither he, nor his words, were in any way responsible for them."

"I'm sure he will be relieved to hear that, miss," the innkeeper replied. He hesitated. He continued. "Is there anything I can do?"

"No," Lyssa said. "The matter is resolved now."

"Well, I'm thankful for that!"

Lyssa stood upright and turned to look directly into his eyes. The savage, brilliant green almost overwhelmed him and he stepped back, his own eyes wide. "Be careful what you give thanks for." For a moment her voice was biting cold, as brutal as an avalanche in the mountains, as heartless as a demon from the deepest pits of hell. Then the moment was gone. She took coin from her pouch. "I shall be away for a while. Probably a week or so. Can I pay in advance to reserve the room in case I need it again?"

"Er ..." the innkeeper was still recovering "... of course, miss."

She handed him the coinage. "I reserve the room for a week. If I am not back by then I shall not be coming back. Will that suffice?"

He looked down at his hand. "That is more than sufficient, miss. Much more."

"Then consider any extra a recognition of your fine inn and excellent service," Lyssa said. She picked up her bags and strode from the inn without further word. Once outside she collected her horse and rode out of the city, stopping only once on the way, at the same shop she had bought her two previous maps. This time she purchased one that showed the city's nineteen public wells.

The first call was the dragon on watch. Now that she knew the way she rode through the rest of the day and well into the night. It was about midnight when she tethered her horse and climbed the last couple of miles on foot. Once more she found a watch dragon and introduced herself.

"There's a horse just down the track," she informed him. "If you fancy a snack you're welcome to him."

It was not something she would have said yesterday. Yesterday she would have felt loyalty to her horse, the beast that had carried her here and served her well, but now she was so fearful of her compassion that she deliberately acted against it. Sacrificing her horse somehow reinforced in her mind the idea that she could sacrifice the people of Tekmir.

The dragon looked at her. "You won't need it to return?"

"What I need now," she assured him, "is to talk to Bhuul in person. I'll have to wait for word to be sent and for him to be free to come here. How long that will be I have no idea, but I certainly can't leave a horse tied to a stone for days on end. Go and eat him, that way he'll do some good. When I need another horse I'll buy one."

The dragon looked at her a moment longer then hauled himself a little up slope to launch into the air. She was buffeted by the gale of his wings for the first three, huge beats. Then he was gone. Lyssa used his absence to pitch a small mountain tent.

The dragon returned. "Rather a small horse," he noted.

"Forgive me," Lyssa replied. "He was a light riding horse. The next time I buy one I shall choose a larger."

"That would be appreciated." The dragon tongue wrapped. "And now, I assume, I am to earn my snack by flying to find Bhuul and tell him you are here?"

"That would also be greatly appreciated," Lyssa confirmed.

Once more the dragon climbed and launched himself, sending Lyssa diving for her tent to support it against the gale of his wings. This time he turned and flew deep into the mountains. Lyssa lit a fire, cooked a meal, and waited. In truth she didn't have to wait long. It was a little after noon the next day when the roar of wings announced the arrival of the queen's battle master.

The massive dragon looked intently at her. "I hear you wished to speak to me in person," he said. "Am I to assume you have significant news for me?"

Lyssa nodded. "I believe I know how to destroy Tekmir."

Bhuul coiled himself at ease on the mountainside and they talked long into the afternoon. Indeed night was beginning to fall by the time he declared himself satisfied. "So where will you get this poison?" he asked.

"There are humans who will sell anything for sufficient gold to weigh down their belt pouches," Lyssa said. "I have names to ask for, and places where I should ask."

"Even if they know you plan to destroy and entire city?"

"I will forget to mention that," Lyssa murmured.

Bhuul considered. "But surely if someone buys sufficient poison to attack a city, then there is little they can be planning to do <u>but</u> attack a city."

"So the people I buy it from will be <u>exceptionally</u> keen not to know what I'm doing with it. That way they can put their hands on their hearts and plead ignorance," Lyssa replied. "That's the way with villainy. The bigger the crime the less the villains want to know. If the crime is huge they want to know nothing at all."

"But still profit from it?"

"Of course," Lyssa said. "Gold in the pouch still weighs as heavy and shines as bright."

Once more she climbed into the crook of Bhuul's claw and he flew her across the mountains.

# Chapter Seven

Molsar Bronn was not a pleasant man, nor a particularly trustworthy one, but at this moment he was most certainly an intrigued one. He stood in an old barn, somewhat broken down, a little outside a small town. In his hand was a golden wheel that he kept flipping, glittering, into the air.

He caught the coin and examined it, addressing it directly. "So, there are another seven hundred and eighteen like you, are there?" Turning, he glanced to a figure standing by the door of the barn. "Any sign of this girl yet, Karda?"

The man by the door shrugged. "Not yet.

"Who have you got out there?"

"Prassan by the road," Karda replied, "and your brother, Salstar, on the roof of the grain store. If anyone comes with her we'll know."

"Make damn sure we do," Molsar growled. "I don't want any unpleasant surprises."

He went back to flipping the coin. Waiting. Half an hour passed, then Karda glanced across at him. "A signal from Salstar. She's on her way."

Once more the coin was caught. "Anything else?"

Karda glanced back outside. "Salstar signals … just one. She's on her own."

"Yeah, maybe," Molsar grumbled, "or whoever is with her knows their business better than Salstar. Always a possibility. When she gets here show her in. Nice as pie, Karda. I don't want to do anything stupid until we know what's going on."

He looked around. A small, folding table. On it a couple of wine goblets and a flask of wine. Two chairs. Not wonderful preparations, but in light of the fact he knew damn all about this girl it was all he could do. He was generally a very wary man, and would normally shy away from anything as unexplained as this, but seven hundred and eighteen golden wheels was a prize that even a cautious man would make a play for.

"I can see her now," Karda said from the door. "She's just ridden into view."

"Describe her."

"Dark hair. Quite long. Slender. Early twenties I would guess, maybe even late teens. Pretty thing. Bright green eyes."

Molsar was unimpressed. "Yeah. Sometimes it's the pretty ones that knife you in the back."

Karda continued to watch, describing. "She has stopped. She dismounts. Tethers her horse. She's looking around."

"Well go and greet her then, Karda," Molsar urged. "Be a good host."

Karda disappeared. There were a few words muffled by distance and walls, then he was back. "In here, miss, if you will." Karda nodded towards Molsar. "Over there."

Lyssa stepped into the barn. It was the first time Molsar had seen her. She was indeed a pretty thing, but the intensity of those green eyes was a little unsettling. For a moment they regarded each other, assessing.

"I assume," Lyssa said, "that I speak to Mr Bronn?"

Molsar nodded. "You do, but you have the advantage of me. Your letter failed to mention your own name."

She laughed. A laugh that was, to Molsar's mind, disturbingly relaxed. "How remiss of me! I really must concentrate more when I write."

Nothing more was forthcoming. "And, perhaps, a second oversight in not giving a name now that you are here?"

She looked directly into his eyes. "Would you believe any name I gave you?"

"No."

Her grin was almost angelic. "Then there is no great point in giving one. Call me whatever you will, Mr Bronn."

Molsar considered a moment, then he too grinned. "You have a certain style, I'll give you that. Alright green eyes, will you join me in a glass of wine before we discuss business?"

"With pleasure." She strode to the table. He poured the wine. He offered the glass and she drained the contents. "Most refreshing after an hour's ride."

Molsar frowned. "How did you know it wasn't drugged or poisoned?"

"I didn't. Was it?"

He chuckled. "As it happens, no, but I am still surprised the idea hadn't occurred to you."

"But it had," she assured him. "As had other facts. I told you in my letter I could make you seven hundred and eighteen golden wheels richer. As I'm sure you're aware I am not carrying that sum on my person at the moment. I therefore assumed you would not be tempted to try drugs or poison yet."

"A valid point," Molsar admitted. "You're certainly not carrying the gold. Not only would that be very stupid, and I don't think you <u>are</u> stupid, but I know the weight of such a sum and you would not be walking as lightly as you do. So, will you sit with me and talk?" He indicated a chair and Lyssa flowed into it. He sat on the other. "Your letter states you wish to buy rat poison."

"Indeed I do."

"Three hundredweight," he added.

She chuckled. "I am troubled by an infestation of vermin."

He considered this statement. "You have one hell of a rat problem if you need to buy this stuff by the cart load."

"There are many of them," she replied, "and they're remarkably big."

He thought a moment. "So why come to me for your rat poison? I'm not … in the business, as it were."

Lyssa leant back in her chair. "Oh, Mr Bronn, you disappoint me! I'd heard you were in <u>any</u> business where a good profit was to be made. Of course if you're unable to supply the goods then ..."

"Did I say that?" he interrupted. "I'm sure, with the assistance of my associates, I could … acquire … what you need, but I am still curious. You offer me seven hundred and eighteen wheels when even three hundredweight of this stuff could be bought from a merchant in the town for ten."

"A merchant in town might ask where the infestation was that required such a quantity."

"And you think I won't?" Molsar growled.

"I think you don't want to know," Lyssa replied. "All you want to know is that your share of seven hundred and eighteen golden wheels will keep you in fine wine and pretty whores for a <u>very</u> long time. Ignorance can be a blessing."

A grin crept onto Molsar's lips. "You're no fool, girl. I'll give you that."

"Aren't I?" Lyssa's voice was light and relaxed. "Surely only a fool would ride, alone and unprotected, into this den of thieves and murderers."

"One moment." Molsar stood and joined Karda at the door. They exchanged whispered conversation. He turned back to Lyssa. "Well, if you have a guardian angel he's good. Damn good. My men haven't spotted him."

Lyssa laughed. "Perhaps I don't have one. You could always make the test."

"And what would I gain by making such a test?"

Lyssa shrugged. "That would depend on whether I was alone and undefended. If I was I guess you would gain me."

Molsar slowly nodded. "Don't think the idea hasn't occurred, green eyes. You're a cute little thing and I'm sure raping you would be very entertaining."

"But ...?"

"What makes you think there's a 'but'?" Molsar asked.

"If there wasn't a 'but'," Lyssa observed, "you wouldn't be talking about it, you'd be doing it."

Molsar grinned. "Fair point. But as you, yourself, said my share of seven hundred and eighteen wheels will keep me in pretty whores for a very long time. You're cute but not <u>that</u> cute. I'll take the gold."

"You'll take the gold and, of course ..." her voice suddenly became harder "... deliver what is paid for."

He fashioned a look of shock and hurt. "As if I would do anything else!"

"I'm glad to hear it," Lyssa said, "and I trust you implicitly. Because of this trust there is no need to warn you that I have friends with very big teeth who would be most ... distressed ... were I to be double crossed."

He tensed. He glared. "Are you threatening me, <u>girl</u>?" His voice was suddenly low and dangerous.

"Yes."

For several seconds he stared into her bright, green eyes. Then a grin slowly spread across his lips, widening and deepening. He tipped back his head and laughter rang out. "Dammit, green eyes, you are at that!" The laughter faded but the mirthful grin remained. "I like you, girl. You've got guts and fire in your belly. You'll go a long way. Alright, if we get the gold you'll get the poison. No questions asked and no silly games. Do we have a deal?"

"We do indeed," Lyssa replied. "Let's shake hands on it, and finish that flask to confirm."

# Chapter Eight

Three days later Lyssa was driving a small cart towards Tekmir. In the back of the cart were nineteen brown sacks, one for each of the city's public wells. Each sack was marked 'rock salt'. With a city high in the mountains, in winter, rock salt for gritting paths was a common commodity. Lyssa had seen many such sacks when she had been in the city. Her own, she suspected, would pass without comment or even thought.

The cart was old. The horse was old. In truth the purchase of the poison had cost Lyssa nearly all the gold that Bhuul and his dragons had managed to acquire for her, but that hardly mattered. The cart would make just one journey and the horse only two, both were sturdy enough for such limited duties. They slowly climbed higher and higher into the mountains. The weather was deteriorating. Heavy snow clouds rolled in, black and threatening. A harbinger of hard times ahead.

For those still alive.

Not only did she have the poison, she had other things she needed. A big, long pair of heavy gloves and a fine, cloth face mask to dampen and tie across her nose and mouth to catch any dust that flew. She didn't want to touch the poison. She didn't want to breath it. In truth she didn't want anything to do with the stuff, but that decision was now long past.

It took ten full days for her aged horse to drag its load through the mountains. Of course Lyssa's reserved room at the inn would be reserved no more, but that didn't matter. She was not planning to spend any more time in the city than she absolutely had to, and for this reason she timed her arrival for just after sunset. As she approached the gate and the gate guard walked towards her her heart hammered in her chest. He flipped away the tarpaulin she had covered the sacks with, read what was written on them, flipped the tarpaulin back and waved her through.

She had even planned her route through the streets from well to well, ensuring she had to cover the least distance in the shortest time, and that she would end near the main gate to make her escape. All she had to do now was wait a while until that quietest of times, about two hours after midnight, and then do the deed. She parked the cart at the side of a little used street, sat in the seat, and waited.

This was it. The last chance to think. The last chance to change her mind. The last chance to turn from one path to another. A last few hours to run through thoughts and arguments so old and familiar that she already knew every nuance of them even before she thought them. The few people who walked past her and saw her sitting on her cart might have thought she was at peace. Little did they understand the chaos in her mind, yet nothing had changed. Nothing could ever change.

Then came the moment. In the quiet and dark she drove the cart to the first well. There she raised water to dampen her mask. She tied it around her face. She donned her long gloves and hauled a sack from the cart to the well lip. She drew her dagger from her belt and held it to the cloth.

There she hesitated. For thirty full seconds the blade hovered, its tip trembling.

"Khaajd! Khaajd! Khaajd! Stop this nonsense! You know you don't have a choice. Just <u>do</u> it!"

The knife sliced, the sack tipped and pale, tawny powder poured. From the well below came a faint hissing noise, gradually fading. It was done. And so, well by well, it was done a further eighteen times. Lyssa took off and discarded her gloves. She took off and discarded her mask. She unhitched the horse from her cart, leaving the cart standing in the deserted street.

The horse was a carthorse in build, but she had managed to find a saddle to fit him. It hardly mattered now, she didn't have far to go. She mounted and headed for the gate …

… and then stopped, and thought, and turned.

Riding as fast as her unsuited mount could carry her she headed for the city centre. There she found a door. She leapt from the saddle and hammered. For several long seconds nothing happened, then a window shutter opened above. Torm's head appeared.

"Leave the city!"

His eyes widened. "What was that?"

"Leave the city! Now! This moment! Take nothing with you, you haven't time. Go!"

Horror swept across his face. "Dear God, Khaajd! What are you going to do?"

"It's not what I'm going to do, it's what I <u>have already done</u>. The city is doomed, Torm. Flee while you can."

He tried to speak. Tried to ask. Tried to understand. She would not let him. Already she was back on her horse and riding to the gate. She passed through never to return as a human, and not in any form while this remained a place of humans.

Following the familiar route she rode into the mountains to the dragon's watch, driving her horse to exhaustion in a quest for speed. There Bhuul waited for her.

"It is done," she told him.

Bhuul looked from her to the city below, now lit by the light of late morning. "So now we wait and watch," he rumbled. "And hope."

"Tell your dragons they must not eat <u>anything</u> within the city," Lyssa warned. "That place is going to be full of humans, dogs, cats, horses, rats and almost every other creature filled with poison."

"They have already been warned," Bhuul assured her. "They understand."

Bhuul called Mhiirak to him, the other dragon was waiting a few miles away, and Mhiirak carried Lyssa back to the mountains. Her work was done. Now it was down to Bhuul and the queen's battle dragons.

Bhuul watched the day unfold, but this day was different to the other days he had watched. There was no bustle in the city below. No crowds in the market square. No river of tiny figures flowing along the streets. He could see the difference. He could sense it. He could almost smell it.

By mid morning the people of Tekmir had started falling sick. First by the hundred, then the thousand. By noon Bhuul started seeing wisps of unfamiliar smoke rising throughout the city, makeshift pyres on street corners as the sick started to die. He smelt the smoke and the distinctive scent of burning flesh. By the time the daylight began to fade the pyres were everywhere and a pall hung over the stricken city.

With a roar of wings Thaakumek landed at his side. "What's happening?" asked the queen of dragons.

"They're dying."

Thaakumek looked from him to the city, then back to him. "So do we just leave them to die?"

"No," Bhuul replied. "The poison will do much but it won't do all. They will be weakened but not destroyed. I shall leave them to die in peace this coming night. Then, with the first light of tomorrow, I shall send in the battle dragons."

Thaakumek looked back at the city. "Will we beat them?"

"If we don't this time," Bhuul replied, "we never shall."

Thaakumek watched for a further half hour, then flew off into the gathering dark. Bhuul remained, his green eyes gleaming like gimlets in the dark. With the morning came three complete wings of dragons, one hundred and eighty, filling the air with their bellows and fury.

Bhuul was under no illusions. Time after time he had lead his dragons against these mountain cities, and time after time they had been beaten back. He had no expectation that Khaajd's poison would, in itself, destroy Tekmir. Only that it might turn the balance from a battle that could not be won into one that could.

Just.

What mattered now was to take this chance, this only chance, this last chance, and make it work. Since he first heard of Khaajd's plan he, too, had been planning. Thinking and preparing. He had six complete wings of battle dragons and a seventh wing that was far from complete. Three hundred and ninety-four dragons, including himself, and that was it. Three hundred and ninety-four against a city of sixty thousand, six thousand of whom were soldiers. A city that had been designed with one thought in mind, to kill his people if they attacked.

He'd spoken to every dragon he commanded. Each one personally. He'd impressed upon them that they couldn't afford to lose a single

<u>life</u> needlessly. If any dragon engaged in stupid heroics, he'd told them, they'd better die doing it. If they didn't he'd flame them himself.

He'd chosen the strongest of his wings, the forth, and swapped dragons in and out from the other wings to make it stronger still. The forth wing was his final weapon. The last drive that would either break the city or be ripped apart by it. In command of the forth he had placed Mhiirak, his most trusted and capable lieutenant, with instructions that they were to remain in the mountains, rested and fresh, until the moment they were needed.

When the first three wings crashed into Tekmir they represented almost half of all the battle dragons Bhuul had, and they flew into the teeth of a savage defence. The air was black with crossbow bolts. From the mountain top he watched the blasts of fire. The dragons charging and being beaten back, plucking crossbow bolts from their thick hides like the stings of bees and then charging again.

The air was full of bellows, roars and the faint hiss of flying missiles.

Certainly at the start it seemed exactly like all the previous occasions they had attacked cities, as if Khaajd's efforts had done nothing at all, and yet it was almost as if Bhuul could sense something. His instinct told him that however ferocious the hail of crossbow bolts that howled from the towers and walls this was not like the other times. Then he had looked down on a city that had radiated certainty and calm, a city that had <u>known</u> itself impregnable. This time he could sense fear. Panic. The realisation that this was a <u>second</u> terrible blow coming immediately after a first.

All they had to do was hold their nerve, not throw lives away, and <u>keep the humans fighting</u>.

Bhuul watched. He pulled the first wing out of the battle early, long before they were exhausted, and replaced them with the fifth. He waited a while longer, then replaced the second with the sixth. Later still he pulled out the third, the last of the original three, replacing them with the first, rested and with their numbers made up from the incomplete seventh.

And so he cycled his battle wings through the battle, removing them before they were exhausted or had suffered enough to make them lose heart. Each time they went back in they were rested and up to full strength, with goats in their bellies and fire in their souls. Change … change … change … but all the time there were three full wings pounding at the city below.

The humans had no such option. A full third of their soldiers were dead. Poisoned. Many more were sick. Also poisoned. Every man they had was in the tower caps or wall galleries. As the morning ebbed away, the afternoon passed, and the light of day began to fade the inevitable happened. The human commanders were forced to pull exhausted men off the defences to snatch something to eat and a few hours of desperately needed sleep. With that the intensity of the defence began to fade.

It was the first time the dragons had ever seen a city weaken. Every previous battle the humans had enjoyed an excess of warriors. They had shifts in place where tired men were replaced by fresh from the barracks. Every previous time the savage intensity of the crossbow fire had never let up, never faltered. But this time it did.

Bhuul tipped back his head and launched brilliant, white signal flame into the darkening sky. A bellow of triumph, yet he could not allow himself to be too triumphant too soon. The battle, he now felt sure, could be won. Yet it could also be lost through stupidity or over enthusiasm. He had seen weakness, but now he had to make that weakness weaker still.

Until now the attack had been almost even, all parts of the outer wall being attacked with equal vigour. Now Bhuul switched his tactics. He instructed his dragons to hurl their greatest efforts at particular points, leaving others under attack but only to the extent needed to keep the defenders busy. The overstretched humans responded by concentrating their efforts where he concentrated his.

Then by moving this point of attack from east to west, from north to south, he forced the humans to keep running.

Through the streets hurried companies of exhausted men, only to arrive where they believed they were needed and be told the desperate need was elsewhere. Again and again the dragons struck, very suddenly and very hard, and were gone.

Above the beleaguered city flew dragons from the wings that were resting. Bhuul did not command them into the air if they would rather rest and eat, but if they wished to fly and drop rocks he was happy for them to do so. Many wished. If they flew, they were told, drop rocks on <u>soldiers</u>. The buildings could wait. The ordinary people could wait. What mattered was killing the guardsmen, so as the hapless defenders ran they found great stones falling on them from above.

Night fell. Dragons are not fundamentally creatures of the night, but can still see well in darkness. In previous city attacks a full day facing everything the city could throw at them had left the dragons tired and dispirited, but this time Bhuul had been so careful his dragons still blazed with fury. Partly because they, like him, could see the change in the city.

This time darkness brought the defenders no relief, no break in which to re-group. Right through the night the dragons kept hitting and moving, hitting and moving. By the cold light of dawn the warriors of Tekmir found that even after twenty-four interminable hours there was no sign of an end in sight.

With dawn came Mhiirak, flying in to join Bhuul at his vantage point. "My wing," he declared, "grows bored sleeping and eating goats while others fight. They know what happens here and want to be part of it."

Bhuul looked at him. "Patience, Mhiirak. The time is not yet right. Let the other wings do the work for now so that you are ready to do your own later."

Mhiirak looked down at the crumbling city. "But look at them!" he complained. "They do nothing! Barely a crossbow bolt!"

"They would do more if we attacked them harder."

"Then let us attack them harder," Mhiirak suggested, "and make them do more."

Bhuul tongue wrapped. "Softly, Mhiirak," he rumbled. "It is not fury that will win this battle for us, it is time. All we have to do is keep them fighting and eventually they will be able to fight no more. Go back to your wing and tell them they will have their chance, and I suspect it will be during this day."

Bhuul's green eyes were fixed on the city below. Mhiirak turned and looked, trying to follow the direction of his battle master's gaze. "What do you look for?"

"I don't know," Bhuul replied. "But when I see it I shall."

Mhiirak returned to his wing and Bhuul watched on. By now, well over a day into furious combat, no amount of cycling his wings could avoid the inevitable. The part seventh wing had been used in full replacing losses in the others. Once this point was reached Bhuul pulled the second from combat and started dismantling that. He was losing dragons, slowly but steadily, and those he still had were getting desperately tired. Even for a dragon over twenty-four hours of combat was taking its toll.

The battle was reaching an end point. Exhausted human fought exhausted dragon. Bhuul watched as the morning slipped away and afternoon settled over the mountains. He needed a breakthrough. He needed it <u>soon</u>.

Then he saw it.

Down at the base of the city's outer wall stood a dragon, slashing and battering at the masonry with his claws. This was not new, but

117

something else was. The dragon was not being struck by crossbow bolts. He stood and attacked unopposed. There was a tiny space, just a few dozen feet of wall, where the overlapping fields of fire from the galleries had failed.

<u>That</u> was the sign Bhuul needed. He swung his head and roared to the mountains behind him. "Mhiirak! The forth wing! Bring them in!" His voice echoed and rumbled, carrying for miles over the mountains. A minute passed. Five. Ten. Then away to the east dots rose above the line of the mountain tops. As the forth wing flew in Bhuul roared to them. "Mhiirak! Look! A dragon attacks the wall unopposed!"

That was all Mhiirak needed. The forth wing crashed into battle. Fresh, unhurt, their hearts filled with fury. Sixty brand new battle dragons, picked by Bhuul to be the best he had, practically swept aside the lone dragon Bhuul had seen earlier and hurled themselves at the city wall. Within the city the alarm went out, the biggest and most vicious of all the attacks they faced had come. Men rushed through the streets, but by now few men and barely able to run. Too little. Far too little. A section of the wall collapsed.

With the wall broken the dragons could now access the unprotected ends of the galleries that adjoined it. Into these they snorted blasts of killing flame, flame that was not, this time, turned aside by steel shutters. Men, burning, fell from the smashed gallery ends.

With the next length of gallery cleared of defenders Mhiirak's dragons could turn their attention to smashing the sections of wall that supported them. Like a row of falling dominoes each section of wall brought down made the next vulnerable. As the wall fell, section by section, the overlapped areas of crossbow fire they provided failed. This, in turn, opened up vulnerabilities in the dragon towers within the city itself. The domino effect spread.

Another effect also spread. Exhausted dragons saw wall collapsing, and with that sight their exhaustion seemed to leave them. Never before had they seen such a thing, but now it happened.

Their eyes shone. Their voices bellowed deep, echoing between the mountains. With energy born of triumph they hurled themselves anew into the fray.

It was still not quick. Right the way though another long, hard, brutal night they fought, but this second night was different. This second night all, dragon and human alike, knew Tekmir was doomed.

Section by section the wall fell. One by one the towers fell. The final one lasted until morning, a forlorn spire surrounded on all sides by a circle of almost two hundred dragons, bathing it in a searing torrent of blue flame while at the base their colleagues clawed and scratched, battered and buffeted.

Bhuul watched that last tower fall. He lifted his head high. "Kill them all!" he bellowed.

The battle dragons needed no such command. They rampaged through the, now defenceless, streets. They ripped open the corners of buildings, ramming their muzzles inside, and unleashed roaring blasts of flame. They shattered walls and collapsed houses. They snapped and crushed and flamed. Those above ground died fast. Those who had sought refuge in their cellars and basements found themselves trapped in the dark under the rubble of buildings above, there to die slowly.

By midnight the destruction was over. No building stood. No house, no hall, no shop, no inn, no wall or tower remained. Just broken stone and brick. Through the rubble stalked dragons, their eyes glittering as they sought things yet to kill. Around the destruction, perched on the mountain tops, their fellows bellowed and launched plumes of brilliant, white signal flame into the night sky. Ink-black, flickering shadows appeared and danced over the fallen stone and brick, then disappeared only to be replaced by another shadow from another direction.

Hell had found its home on earth.

Into this scene, a little after midnight, flew Khaajd, a dragon once more. She landed in the great market square and looked around. Everything was gone, and yet also not gone. Here a smashed doorway retained carvings that reminded her of that same doorway standing. There a handful of bricks still held together to form the corner of a remembered wall. The green and gold canopy under which she had sat and drunk klah lay torn and charred, while the tables and benches were scattered and broken.

The dead were everywhere. Men, women and children. Burned, bitten and crushed. Then there were the other dead. The dead who had not been killed by dragons. The dead whose faces told of last moments of terror and agony. Her own dead. Her own victims. The poisoned. So thick on the ground lay the corpses that Khaajd could not step between. Every stride was accompanied by the sickening crunch of bone, and sudden lubrication underfoot. At first she tried, tried so hard, to avoid the corpses but in the end she had to accept the truth. She had to accept the sensation of literally walking on the dead.

Slowly she made her way from the market square, along streets she knew but could now barely recognise. To the Dragon's Fall inn she went, where she had stayed. The inn built where a dragon had died was now, itself, dead. A dragon looked upon it. Somewhere beneath the rubble would be the innkeeper. Khaajd hoped he was dead. A quick death rather than the lingering fate that would be his if he had taken to his cellar. She looked and turned and went.

Through the streets she walked with neither purpose nor direction. She did not want to see, but was unable to look away.

And then she saw a figure.

How he had been missed by the other dragons she could not guess. Perhaps it was the stillness, or perhaps her own eyes were more accustomed to recognising the human form. Atop a pile of rubble a man sat, still in the flickering of dragon light, a shadow on top of a shadow. For a moment she thought he must be dead, one corpse among so many, yet no dead man sits thus.

He leant forwards, in his arms a wrapped bundle.

She approached and he heard her. His head rose and his eyes looked into her own. For a moment they regarded each other in silent stillness. A human. An enemy of her people. A survivor in a shattered city. All of these things. With a snort of flame he would be gone. With a snap of her jaws or the merest touch of claw. Yet she did not kill. She couldn't.

"I haven't seen you," she rumbled in human speech, and turned away.

She took one step, then another, then something struck behind her ear flap and a howl of fury erupted behind her. "You haven't seen me? You haven't seen me?" Whipping her head round she instinctively flinched as a rock flew past. The man was stooping to pick up another missile, his bundle held in one arm. Another rock flew. And another. "Well perhaps you can see me now!"

His voice was like no other she had ever heard. A howl of limitless hatred mixed with utter despair. "And perhaps you see this!" He brandished the bundle he held. "My daughter. She's dead. My wife. Dead. My son. Dead. Everyone is dead. See me, dragon! See everything and know what you and your kind have done!"

Almost reverently he lowered the bundle to the rubble and grasped a handy lump of timber. He hurled himself at Khaajd's feet. "Damn you! Curse you! Curse you all!"

Rocks meant nothing, a thrown stone merely bounces off a dragon. The timber swung at her feet meant nothing, she would hardly feel the blows. She found herself assaulted by an insect, insignificant and incapable of harm. With a stamp or bite or sneeze it would all be over, and yet she still couldn't kill. She shuffled backwards, pulling her feet away from his fury, then turned and fled.

It was not his physical attack that hurt her, but hurt she was. It was his voice that pierced her heart. A voice of infinite pain that flooded

121

into her and became her own pain. She could not face his despair. His loss. And what she had done.

His voice pursued her through the darkness. "Burn in hell!" he screamed. "Burn in hell!"

Yet she was already in hell, and already burning. She fled five or six hundred yards before she recovered enouigh composure to stop, but even at this distance she could still hear him raging. Then came another sound, the voice of a dragon. "Ah. Here is one that yet lives. What? He shouts at me and throws stones at my head!"

There was the loud, savage roar of killing flame. Even at this distance Khaajd could still feel the heat. Then, once more, came silence.

She stood, frozen. Her neck arched and her muzzle just a fraction from the ground. Burn in hell. Light flared and she saw, in the dust, a flash of colour. A speck of blue amid the brown and grey of the dust. She snorted it clean to reveal the one thing in this entire city she could not bear to find.

It was Mr Dog.

# Chapter Nine

The next day Khaajd stood in the heart of the mountains, her neck arched, her head low, looking at her reflection in a pool among the rocks. Memories haunted her. However hard she tried she could not get sounds, sights and voices out of her head. The voices of the dead.

Up you get, deary.

Around her the mountains were full of celebration, and had been since the moment Tekmir fell. Dragons sat on mountain tops warbling with delight and hurling joyous flame into the sky. The sense of impending, inevitable, slow doom that had seeped into her people's hearts was lifted. They dared to hope again. They believed.

Yet did Khaajd believe? Did she think what had happened at Tekmir had bought them anything at all? No, not really. The other cities still flourished in the mountains and more were being built. Cities that knew Tekmir had been poisoned, destroyed from within. Whatever she had done in Tekmir she would not be able to do elsewhere.

Nor could she bare to. The deaths of sixty thousand people rested heavily on her. For Bhuul and his battle dragons they were just enemies. Faceless, nameless, characterless creatures to be attacked and killed. For her they were people. Real people with hearts and souls. The green eyes that looked up at her out of the water were troubled, sorrowful and full of self accusation.

Burn in hell!

Reaching out a massive claw she softly raked the surface of the water. Ripples spread and her reflection broke into a myriad of scattered shards. Slowly the water stilled and the reflection reassembled itself yet nothing had changed. The eyes were still filled with horror. The eyes of a creature haunted, with no hope of escape from the guilt that assaulted her.

Say thank you to the pretty lady.

The water exploded in front of her. Without thought, without intention, almost without realisation she struck at the pool and her own reflection. Again and again she struck. Again and again the water plumed and frothed.

"It's not a good sign ..." The voice froze her, her claw poised between one stroke and the next. "... striking at your reflection in the water. Not a good sign at all."

Khaajd looked up and found Thaakumek gazing at her. For a moment she remained frozen, then she lowered her claw to the ground. "No," she admitted. "It isn't."

"You need time," Thaakumek said. "Bhuul wants to take our success at Tekmir and repeat it at another mountain city. He urges me to send you out again into the human world, and do so soon before the humans can learn what happened at Tekmir. I told him you were not ready."

"I will never be ready," Khaajd murmured.

Thaakumek considered these words. "That I feared," she replied, "but I didn't tell Bhuul of my fear. He argued strongly that we need to strike again and soon, and urged me to allow him to speak with you personally in the hope of persuading you. I refused him that permission and instructed him that you were not to be disturbed or bothered in any way until I, myself, told him you were ready for such an approach."

"Did he agree?"

"Of course he agreed." Thaakumek seemed almost affronted. "I am queen and my words hold weight. He is not happy, but he is loyal and accepts my authority. He will leave you alone."

Khaajd's eyes were drawn, once more, to her reflection. "Then, for that, you have my sincere thanks."

She heard the sound of movement. The scrape of heavy scale on hard rock. The grind and catch of claw. Then she felt the warmth of breath and the touch of a muzzle behind her left ear. "Take your time, Khaajd," the queen said. "Fly through the mountains. Eat goats. Lounge in icy pools. Breathe the fresh air of your homeland, the homeland your efforts have helped to defend. Learn to enjoy being a dragon again."

"And then?"

"And then," Thaakumek said, "you must decide what to do. Bhuul believes we must continue the fight, destroying more cities as we destroyed Tekmir. Yet only you can know if you are capable of doing so."

Khaajd paused a moment. "It's not as simple as that," she said, "even if I had no doubts and no reluctance. Tekmir fell because they expected to be attacked by dragons and never saw a human as a danger. The lesson has now been learned. The humans would be ready for me next time. They will watch their wells, and watch all the other things I might find vulnerable. They now <u>know</u> they were betrayed."

"What might they know?" Thaakumek asked. "That the people of Tekmir were poisoned, perhaps, if they managed to get message out of the city before Bhuul's dragons attacked."

Khaajd almost tongue wrapped. "Of that there will be no doubt <u>at all</u>. Message pigeons would have been flying out of Tekmir from the moment the first people started to fall sick. The people of the other cities will know <u>everything</u> that Tekmir itself could discover. They will probably know the poison was brought into the city by cart, in sacks labelled 'Rock Salt', by you young woman with dark hair and brilliant green eyes. They will probably know that I travelled under the name of Lyssa Urdak and stayed at the Dragon's Fall inn. They might even have discovered who I bought the poison from and how much I paid for it."

Thaakumek considered. "Which means ...?"

"Which means I would not last five minutes if I were to try and walk into another city as a human. They would take one look at my age, my dark hair and my green eyes, and I would find myself in chains, being taken away for questioning. Whatever else may happen my days of working in secrecy among the humans are gone, never to return."

Thaakumek's head dropped a fraction. "That is bad news indeed," she said. "Bhuul will be greatly disappointed."

"And you, Thaakumek?" Khaajd asked. "Will you, too, be 'greatly disappointed'?"

The queen considered her reply. "I have one desire that overrides all. The driving desire that rules my life and directs my every thought. I must do all within my power to save my people from slow death and extinction."

"I guess that means 'yes'."

"It means 'yes'," Thaakumek admitted, "but that is of little note now. Whether yes or no you remain unready for any further work against the humans. For now you are a dragon. For the future it appears you may have to remain a dragon. I will speak to Bhuul."

"And I shall continue striking at my reflection in the water."

For a full minute the dragon queen looked at her. "Forgive me, Khaajd. I knew you felt doubt and distress, but I was unaware of just how much."

"You cannot live among a people for over twenty years," Khaajd replied, "without coming to know them. When you come to know humans you find they are not evil. Well, some are but the majority are not. Neither are the majority cruel or heartless. Sometimes they're stupid, sometimes selfish and unthinking, often preoccupied with their own lives, sometimes moody or angry or prejudiced, but on the whole they're not a bad race. They're just, well, ordinary people getting on with living their lives. Then you find the occasional one who is exceptional. The occasional one who thinks and understands. A human who is not afraid to dream wonderful dreams and think wonderful thoughts. There was one in Tekmir, his name was Torm and he was the humans' expert on all matters of dragonkind."

"Then one human at least I grieve for," Thaakumek murmured. "This 'Torm' will be a loss."

"Or hopefully not," Khaajd replied. "I warned him of the impending destruction of Tekmir early in the morning when I had just poisoned the wells. I told him the city was doomed and urged him to flee. I don't know if he did."

Thaakumek tongue wrapped. "I'm not sure if I approve of you warning the humans in advance of our attack," she said, "but in light of what you say I shall, on this occasion, forgive you. Let's hope he heeded your warning and escaped while he could." The queen left Khaajd in peace, flying off into the mountains. Khaajd, once more, returned to gazing at her face in the water.

# Chapter Ten

Time passed. Days became weeks, weeks became months and the snow of winter vanished under the sun of spring and summer. Yet snow was not all that melted away. The euphoria of victory also faded from the dragons of the mountains. The great triumph of Tekmir drifted from being present to being recent, and finally to not being recent either.

In the mountains four other human cities thrived, their walls as strong and their towers as high as Tekmir's had been. Two further continued to be built to replace the one that was gone. The summer came and went, warmth cooling to the biting cold of another winter, and despair crept again into the hearts of dragons. One city had been destroyed but it made no difference at all. Unless that one victory could be followed by others they remained doomed. Tekmir would become a single triumph, a single moment of cruel, false hope, before the dragons were slowly, remorselessly, mercilessly crushed into non-existance.

Thaakumek saw the despair and understood it. She also felt it in her own heart. Almost exactly a year after Tekmir fell she flew, once more, to speak with Khaajd at her cave.

"Khaajd?" Khaajd raised her head and turned it to her queen. Thaakumek was shocked. Khaajd was a bare shadow of her former self with ribs standing proud, muscles wasted and her neck thin and weak. A dragon starving, and obviously so. In an instant the dragon queen set aside one concern for another, her thoughts switching from the troubles of her people to the troubles of one alone. "Khaajd! Are you sick?"

"Yes." The voice was as weak as the body, "but not with any sickness you can aid. I cannot sleep without being haunted by the voices and faces of those I murdered. I have no desire to hunt, and when I force myself to do so I end up with a dead goat I have even less desire to eat. I force myself to eat as well, even when I do not desire it, but not as much as I should. In truth I wish I had not been a coward. How much better it would have been if, after poisoning the last well at Tekmir, I had drawn water and drunk my fill? Then, at least, my head would not be filled with nightmares."

Thaakumek could hardly believe the evidence of her own eyes and ears. She had known Khaajd was troubled by what she had done at Tekmir, but this talk of wishing her own death was beyond all expectation. As was the condition she found Khaajd in, half starved and desperately weak. "What a fool I've been," she murmured. "I left you alone believing you needed time and solitude to heal, but I never realised how deep the pain ran. Just how <u>much</u> harm had been done. You deserved better of your queen."

"I deserved nothing and deserve nothing." Khaajd's voice was bitter with self loathing. "I am a poisoner of children, a butcher of the innocent, a slaughterer of the honest and decent. I am the foulest creature to have ever drawn breath. The souls of sixty thousand dead scream for vengeance, and every one of them deserves it in full."

"Not in my eyes," murmured the queen.

"Your eyes do not count!" Khaajd snapped, for the first time ever raising her voice in anger to her queen.

"True, they do not," Thaakumek admitted, her voice soft. "Yet you are a dragon and I am the queen of dragons. I am responsible for your welfare as I am any other dragon. What is more you are my friend, and the dragon to whom I owe so much. I have neglected that friendship and debt. I will hunt for you, Khaajd. I will personally hunt for you, and bring you five goats each day if I have to scour every mountainside for a hundred miles to find them. I need you well and strong. We all need you well and strong."

"For what?" Khaajd asked. "What use am I now, to you or any other dragon? I was your weapon among the humans but now I am a broken weapon. I can never do again what I did at Tekmir, it would tear me apart."

"That may be the case ..."

"It is the case," Khaajd interjected. "I am finished. Done. Spent. I have nothing left to give, and my only desire is to survive whatever is left of my life without being driven to insanity by the guilt that rages in my head. If the rest of my life happens to be short it will be a relief to all, not least to me."

Thaakumek looked at her long and hard. "Goats," she said and started to unfurl her wings.

"Do not trouble yourself ..."

"Enough!" Thaakumek snapped in sudden anger. "What I choose to trouble myself with is my concern. While you may be prepared to wallow in self-pity and loathing, slowly starving yourself to death, I am not prepared to let you. I will bring you goats and you will eat them. That is the end of the matter. Understood?"

Khaajd looked at her. "I have no choice?"

"Not unless you would defy the direct command of your queen," Thaakumek growled. "Will you do that, Khaajd? Will you disobey me?"

Khaajd looked into her queen's blazing, green eyes. "No," she whispered. "I have not done so in the past. I will not start now."

Thaakumek's ire vanished like mist in a gale, leaving behind her own shadow of guilt. "Forgive me, Khaajd," she murmured. "I had no right to speak in anger to one I have hurt so."

"You did not hurt me."

"Yes I did," Thaakumek replied. "You didn't destroy Tekmir by my command, but you certainly destroyed it at my wish and because of the promise you made to me. That is enough. I will not command you. Never again. For as long as we both live you will always be free to do, or not do, as your heart tells you. Whatever you want shall be, and I shall stand beside you as a friend not a queen. Now will you please let me hunt you some goats?"

Khaajd took a deep breath. "When I spoke to Torm in Tekmir I told him I served a fine and noble queen. I wasn't wrong. Very well, Thaakuumek, if catching me some goats would please you then it would honour me. Few indeed have had the queen of dragons hunt for them and this will be my second occasion." Thaakumek tilted her head, puzzled. "You hunted a goat for me when I changed back into a human," Khaajd reminded. "Before I went to Tekmir. I roasted it over a fire and offered you some."

Thaakumek remembered the occasion. "I refused it. It smelled somewhat foul if I recall. Are you planning to roast your goats this time?"

Khaajd tongue wrapped. "No, my days of roasting goats are over now. I shall never again be a human."

"You're sure?"

"Yes I am." Khaajd's reply was soft but certain. "Being a human has brought me as much pain as I can bear. In fact more than I can bear. No more. Not ever. From now on I live or die as a dragon."

Thaakumek once more unfurled her wings. She launched herself into the air. Khaajd watched her circle and climb into the winter sky above, then set off in search of prey. As it happened she didn't need to scour the mountains for a hundred miles, goats were relatively plentiful. Within a couple of hours she was back with five of good size.

Khaajd still found she had no appetite, but by sheer force of will she managed to eat all she was brought. Then she settled on the mountainside and Thaakumek settled beside her.

"So why are you here?" Khaajd asked.

"It doesn't matter now."

"Oh, but it does," Khaajd replied. "When the queen of dragons flies far through the mountains she does so with purpose. You are not here by accident, or to catch me goats, you had something else on your mind. Some matter of importance."

"Yes," Thaakumek admitted. "I had a matter in mind. Something to ask of you, but something I now know you cannot possibly do."

That was all the explanation Khaajd needed. "Destroy another city?"

"I'd hoped, but it is not to be. That's clear now." Thaakumek said. "We are doomed and I do not know how to turn that fate aside. Our only hope was to make the humans fear us again, but they do not fear us. We had only one weapon, you, and that weapon is now gone. The humans know this. My fate is to be the queen that fails my people, and has to watch them die."

"You have not failed the dragons."

"What else can it be called?" Thaakumek asked.

Khaajd didn't answer. Instead she lay on the rocks, thinking. "There are four cities, and two more being built."

"There were five," Thaakumek murmured. "Now, briefly, four. Soon there will be six, then eight, then ten, then fifteen, and so it will continue."

Khaajd thought back to her time as a human, pulling names and details from a reluctant memory. "Molsin is small, barely ten thousand. Next comes Luss Bennek with, perhaps, twice that number ..."

"The size doesn't matter," Thaakumek interjected. "What matters is that we can do nothing. However small or large they are, they will always stand safe from everything we can throw at them."

Khaajd glanced at her queen but carried on as if she hadn't spoken. "... Aldenar is similar in size to Tekmir, perhaps sixty thousand. Biggest of them all is Yullat. It may have been established after Tekmir but has grown much faster since. I've never been there but I am told it's a vast place, inhabited by over two hundred thousand."

"There is indeed one that is huge," Thaakumek confirmed. "I have flown to it many times with Bhuul and seen its hugeness with my own eyes."

"It is in Yullat that the duke lives."

"Ah yes, their ruler," Thaakumek murmured. "You mentioned him when you first returned from the human world."

A strange feeling crept over Khaajd. An odd sense of ... fate. "Will you fly with me, Thaakumek?"

It was not what the dragon queen expected. She turned to look at Khaajd, puzzled. "Fly with you? Of course I'll fly with you, but to where?"

"To Yullat."

Thaakumek's puzzlement increased. "Why? What is there at Yullat, except for a vision of the future for the mountains? A vision of our own doom?"

"I don't know," Khaajd replied, and truly she didn't. "I just ..." Her voice trailed away as she found she had no words to express herself, or perhaps had no coherent thoughts to express. Even she didn't know which. "... I just want to see."

"Then see you shall," Thaakumek murmured. "Rest well tonight. Sleep deep. I shall stay with you, and while I may not be able to chase away your nightmares at least you will know you're not alone. Tomorrow I will catch you more goats and you will eat, for you will need strength for the flight. It is no short distance. Then we shall fly to Yullat and see ... well ... whatever there is to see."

True to her word Thaakumek kept watch as Khaajd drifted into a fitful and disturbed sleep.

The next morning Khaajd woke to the sound of wings as Thaakumek launched herself from the ridge above. "I go to catch goats!" the queen called. "Go and drink. Make sure you have an appetite by the time I return!" Then she was gone.

Khaajd levered herself to her feet, stretching and twisting neck, wings, legs, tail and torso to banish the stiffness of sleep from her body. A stiffness she had experienced little of late. This morning, for the first time in many mornings, she woke without a lingering exhaustion hanging over her.

She felt ... different. The demons of her dreams had, indeed, been easier to face knowing she had a friend at her side.

There was something else as well. Yesterday the words she had both spoken and heard had been largely words of despair and doom, but with the new day had come a new lightness of heart. A sense that

135

all was <u>not</u> ill, and hope remained for her, her queen and her people. It had been a moment of bizarre inspiration that had lead her to suggest a flight to Yullat, yet now a new day confirmed that inspiration. Dragons were not a people given to superstition, so perhaps it was the part of her steeped in human experience that spoke to her. Whatever the reason she felt a new optimism in her heart, and with that even the light of the day seemed brighter and kinder.

For Thaakumek the hunting was easy, and for this she gave thanks as she was now hunting for two. Despite this it still took her three hours to find eight goats. Three for herself, which she bolted down with unseemly haste, and the other five for Khaajd. By the time she returned it was already well over half way through the short, winter morning. By the time Khaajd had eaten and drunk her fill that morning would be gone.

Almost five hundred leagues through and above the mountains lay between them and Yullat. Not a long flight for a dragon in good condition, but not insignificant. For a dragon weakened and malnourished it would be challenging indeed, yet Thaakumek was pleased and encouraged to see Khaajd showing signs of enthusiasm and good spirits when she returned with the five goats. When the goats were eaten with no need of encouragement she was more pleased still. A good sign.

The meal consumed they climbed high on the ridge and launched themselves, weaving between the mountains until they could climb above them. For Khaajd it was, indeed, a challenging flight. In truth she hadn't fully appreciated just how weak she was. How her body, though too light, seemed as heavy as lead to her lifeless, aching wings.

Thaakumek allowed Khaajd to lead and set her own pace. The queen simply followed and watched, noting how her companion took far longer than she would have expected to gain height. When Khaajd eventually levelled out she was barely higher than the highest mountain tops, the draft from her wings flicking snow off the rocks, and at least five thousand feet lower than any healthy dragon would have flown.

The dragon queen beat her wings harder and was, within a couple of minutes, flying alongside. "How are you, Khaajd?"

"Would you believe if I said I had never felt better?"

Thaakumek could hear the effort in her voice. "No." The answer was direct and truthful.

"Then I shall be honest," Khaajd said. "Flying is an effort, and more then I thought it would be. I am weaker than I believed, but I am in no danger of falling from the sky and would land before I were."

"Good," Thaakumek replied. "Then lead and I shall follow. If you need to land, land. The humans may be building their cities but I doubt it will make any difference if we take three hours or three days to reach Yullat. Even humans manage little in that time."

Thaakumek dropped back and followed, watching, while Khaajd flew on. As it happened Khaajd didn't need to land and rest, but it was a closer matter than she would have willingly admitted to her queen. By the time she saw the distant lights of Yullat shining in the darkening afternoon she had remarkably little strength left to give. The final long, slow glide down to a landing was a welcome relief from the effort of maintaining height.

She struggled to cup her wings and slow her speed, managed it only to a partial extent, and crumpled onto the ground in an ungainly, but thankfully unharmed, heap. Thaakumek landed beside her in much more dignified fashion.

"Perhaps a triumph of stubbornness over wisdom?" the queen asked.

Khaajd got her legs under her and furled her wings. "I landed before I fell from the sky, as I promised I would do." She looked towards Yullat.

Beneath them the city spread in the growing gloom. A gleaming, glittering jewel of shimmering lamps and lanterns. A network of illuminated roads and paths filled the valley in which the vast city was built. Within the mesh of roads rose buildings, their windows radiant.

It was the sheer <u>size</u> of the city that assailed Khaajd's mind. Tekmir had been built within a city wall, and basically remained within it for a hundred years. Admittedly the early Tekmir had contained a great deal of empty space, and as time had past the human population had grown steadily denser, but Tekmir's growth had been slow.

Yullat, on the other hand, had grown much faster, rapidly reaching and surpassing the population of its older sister city. Six times it had become necessary to expand the total area by building new lengths of city wall, containing new dragon towers, which swept out from the original walls and back in a huge arc. Petals on a vast, suburban flower.

The result dwarfed the late Tekmir. Khaajd had heard of a population of two hundred thousand for this place but, now that she could see it with her own eyes, she could not believe a figure so low. Surely there had to be three or even four hundred thousand people down there! Even for a dragon it was an awesome sight, and especially for a dragon a terrifying one.

The light of day was fading, and as the sunlight ebbed the lights of the city shone ever brighter and stronger. Khaajd turned her head this way and that, scanning the scene in front of her.

"That," Thaakumek murmured, "is the future of the mountains, and for all my fears and sorrows I have to admit they do it well."

"Everything they turn their minds to they do well," Khaajd replied. "That is the nature of humans. That is what makes them so deadly. Whatever is not to their liking they change until it suits them better, whatever it may be." As the sun finally dipped below the line of the western mountains Khaajd became aware of another line of light in the distance. She prodded her nose in its direction. "What is that?"

Thaakumek turned and looked. "Ah, yes. Bhuul has shown me that before. The humans have built a great wall between the arms of the mountain higher up the valley. A wall behind which the water gathers to form a vast lake."

"A wall holding back water," Khaajd mused. "Yes, I have heard of them but not seen one. They call it a dam. May I go and see?"

Thaakumek looked at her. "You are here to see anything and everything you wish," she replied, "and remain as long as you desire."

Khaajd felt she had rested just long enough to test her strength with another take off, so she spread her wings and hurled herself into the air. Flapping wearily she flew towards the distant line of light.

# Chapter Eleven

From the window of a darkened room in the city below she was observed. Duke Telchar Bliss stood, his hands clasped behind his back, watching the dragons that watched them. There was a knock at the door behind him and he half turned his head. "Come." His was a deep voice. Resonant. Crisp. A voice used to the issue of command. There was a brief flare of light in the room as a door opened, and then darkness returned as it closed again.

"You sent for me, my Lord?"

The duke turned back to the window. "Yes indeed, Farron. Join me if you will." Lord Farron joined his duke at the window and both looked out. "Two dragons," the duke continued. "Not big ones. In fact rather small, certainly not the battle dragon type. There ..." He pointed. "... is one that sits and watches us. The other has flown off up the valley ..." He opened the window and leaned out to peer. "... Yes. The other is up by the dam, looking at it. What do you make of them?"

Farron chuckled. "Well, one I can name my lord, and we are truly honoured. That beast ..." He nodded in the direction of the nearer dragon. "... is their queen, Thaakumek."

"Is she, by God!" The duke turned his attention back to the nearer dragon, viewing her with renewed interest. "Honoured indeed, Farron. She is known to us, then?"

"There is a huge, male battle dragon," Farron said by way of an explanation. "A beast called Bhuul who oversaw the slaughter at Tekmir. The queen is often seen with him, overlooking our cities and discussing matters, so yes she is known to us. There is talk that there may be some connection between her and Bhuul beyond that of queen and commander of soldiers though, in truth, I have heard no evidence to support such rumour. I suspect it is little more than the fanciful imagination of bored soldiers."

The duke glanced at Farron. "Mates? Partners?"

"So the tales would have it, my lord," Farron said, "yet there seems no real evidence to support such speculation."

The duke turned his attention back to the window and the dragon beyond, now lit almost entirely by bright moonlight. "Yet she is not here with a great brute of a battle dragon this time, is she Farron?"

"Indeed she isn't," Farron confirmed. "The other is another female, but she looks far from well. A thin, half starved creature from what we can see, despite being obviously young."

Again the duke leant out of the window to view the more distant dragon by the dam. "A strange companion, wouldn't you say, for a great and powerful queen?"

Farron nodded. "Strange indeed, and she's completely unknown to us. Of course we see far less of the females than we do of the battle dragons, they tend to stay deep within the mountains and far away from us, but I admit to being curious about this one."

The duke rocked back and forth between the toes and heels of his boots. "A thought occurs to me. There is <u>one</u> other female dragon that we most certainly know about."

"The bi-form that poisoned the Tekmir wells?"

The duke nodded. "That's the one. Might she not be just the companion chosen by the queen to accompany her and discuss further death and slaughter?"

"Indeed," Farron said, though his voice suggested doubt.

Again the duke glanced at him. "You don't buy that theory?"

Farron shrugged his shoulders non-committally. "I'm surprised at this female's poor condition," he said. "Surely the poisoner of Tekmir would have been hailed a heroine and fed goats until they came out of her ears, not appear as this thin, weak shadow of a creature."

"Perhaps she got a lungful of her own poison as she poured it into the Tekmir wells," the duke suggested. "Maybe that's why we haven't seen her until now, she nearly died and is still far from well and strong."

"We can hope," Farron said, an edge of viciousness in his voice.

For a couple more minutes the duke continued to watch in silence. "Ah! The one that flew to the dam returns to her queen. I think they speak ..." He tilted his head at the open window, listening intently. "... Yes, even at this distance I hear the faint rumble of the dragon tongue." He thought a moment. "Farron, there was that man who escaped from Tekmir the night of the poisoning? The one who told us of the bi-form in the city?"

"Torm, my Lord?" Farron answered questions with questions. "The dragon expert?"

"That's the man," the duke confirmed. "Where is he at the moment?"

"He's staying as a guest at the guard barracks attached to this palace."

The duke turned, a frown on his face. "A guest at the barracks?"

"For his own safety, my lord," Farron explained. "Once it became known that he had been aware of the bi-form in Tekmir, and not informed the authorities, many began to question his loyalties. The last thing we wanted was him strung up by a mob."

The duke nodded. "Indeed. Yet for now I would like to speak to the man and hear his views on these dragons. Could you find him for me?"

"At once, my lord."

Farron bowed and left. The duke, once more, turned to the window and the dragons beyond. "Stay just where you are, queen of dragons," he murmured into the darkness, "until Mr Torm has had a chance to see you."

Thankfully the two dragons seemed in no hurry to leave. They stayed perched on a ridge above the city, and every now and then the deep rumbling of dragon speech wafted to the ears of the listening duke. In the end it took some fifteen minutes for Farron to return with the guardsmen's guest. Farron ushered Torm into the room and made the necessary introductions. The niceties over, the duke invited Torm to join him at the window.

"Look," the duke said, pointing. "Dragons. Your speciality, I believe."

Torm stepped closer to the window, peering intently in the moonlight. "I wish it were day so I could see them more clearly," he murmured. "Certainly two females, both relatively young. One is in prime condition, the other most certainly not. I can see her ribs. Long illness, perhaps?"

"The healthy beast is the queen of dragons," the duke said.

"Ah! Thaakumek? Well, well!" Torm looked intently. "I have seen her before, but only at great distance unfortunately. She certainly appears a fine specimen, yet who is the weakened dragon?"

"We don't know. I wondered if she might be your bi-form."

"Khaajd?" Torm glanced to the duke then back to the scene outside. "Dear God, I hope not. She looks far from well."

"Can you see anything to either strengthen or weaken my guess?" the duke asked.

"I ..." Torm frowned. "... I can't really help you much there, my lord. I never saw Khaajd as anything but a human. Then she appeared as a beautiful young woman of, perhaps, some twenty years."

"There is some connection between the age of a bi-form dragon and the age they appear when in human form?" the duke asked.

"By all accounts, yes," Torm said. "A young dragon changes into a young human. An old dragon changes into an old human. The two forms always indicate a similar stage in life."

"So if Khaajd looked twenty as a human then it would indicate that she was a young adult dragon?"

"Certainly," Torm confirmed, "and that female is certainly young, even if not in good health. The age might well be about right."

The duke nodded. "So while the guess isn't confirmed, it isn't disproved either." He rocked on his feet half a minute. "Gentlemen. Let us make a working assumption that what we're looking at here is Thaakumek, queen of dragons, accompanied by her faithful servant, spy and poisoner of wells, Khaajd. What are they doing <u>here</u>, looking at our city and dam?"

"Planning our deaths," came Farron's reply.

145

Torm frowned. The expression was not missed by the duke. "You have another theory, perhaps, Torm?"

"Well," Torm replied hesitantly, "not a theory, as such, just doubt about the one offered. If Thaakumek and Khaajd were planning an attack against Yullat wouldn't the queen's battle master, Bhuul, also be present? It is he that commands the wings and he that knows battle."

The duke considered and nodded. "A fair point," he conceded, and turned to Farron. "Get a message to every tower and gallery in the city, Farron. I want to know if Bhuul has been <u>anywhere</u> within sight of Yullat in the last week. I don't care how briefly, or who he was with, I just want to know if he's showing us any interest at all."

"As you command, my lord." Farron left.

Outside the window the two dragons spread their wings and launched themselves into the night sky. Torm and the duke watched them circle for height before disappearing.

"What in the name of hell are you up to, queen of dragons?" murmured the duke to the empty mountains.

# Chapter Twelve

---

Thaakumek and Khaajd didn't fly far. Khaajd was in no state to reach her cave so they just moved from the immediate vicinity of the city and settled for the night. In truth a cave is never a necessity to a dragon, even on the coldest winter night with a blizzard raging, but more of a comfort and a place to call home. Dragons could, indeed often did, sleep in the open under winter skies.

"I'll catch more goats for you in the morning," Thaakumek promised, "though it may take a lot longer. Goats are rare in these parts. They like human company no more than we do."

"They like our company even less," Khaajd observed, tongue wrapping.

"True," agreed Thaakumek, "as I would in their place. So what did you see at Yullat, Khaajd?"

"Nothing you did not see yourself."

"Then that was nothing of value," Thaakumek murmured. "I feared as much, that this visit would prove without purpose."

Khaajd looked at her queen. "It has not proved without purpose yet," she observed. "Thaakumek, have you ever been filled with a … <u>feeling</u> … I can think of no other word for it … that something significant is about to happen?"

Thaakumek tilted her head. "No," she confessed, "I have not. You have such a feeling now?"

"Stronger with every passing hour," Khaajd replied. "Back at my cave, when I asked you to fly here with me, it was just faint. Vague and distant. Now it's immediate and impending as if something creeps up on us. Something bigger than us, bigger than the humans, bigger than everything."

Thaakumek considered these words. "I'm not sure I find that comforting. I would rather be the dragon to other goats, than the goat to some other dragon! What nature of thing do you feel?"

"I don't know," Khaajd replied, "but we must be here when it arrives. Not in my cave, or in yours, but here at Yullat. I know it. Don't ask me how I know but this is where it will happen, whatever it is."

Thaakumek considered. "I have never been one for hunches of feelings," she said, "but in the absence of other options I will take whatever is offered to me. If your feeling tells you we must remain here then here we will remain until either the feeling fades or it proves justified. Now sleep, Khaajd. Rest as best you can. I shall watch over you."

Khaajd lowered her head to the stone and closed her eyes. She didn't know how long she had slept, but when she woke again it was with a sudden start. Unsure of what had suddenly sprung wakefulness upon her she lifted her head and looked around. A short distance away Thaakumek was also awake and intensely alert, her neck twisting and her head swivelling as she looked first this way then that.

"What has just happened?" Khaajd didn't need confirmation that <u>something</u> had happened, of that she was sure, she just didn't know what it was.

"The mountain moved," Thaakumek replied.

"Moved?"

"Yes," the queen confirmed. "A sudden, sharp movement, a clattering of rocks, then nothing."

"But mountains don't move ..."

"This one did," Thaakumek interrupted. "Not just this one either, I believe. They all moved."

"I don't understand," Khaajd began. "How can mountains ..." Her words were cut short. The stone beneath her body shifted. She felt it shift. A slow lift followed by a sudden drop, down and to one side. Her eyes widened. "... move like that?"

"That one was stronger than the first," Thaakumek said. "A bigger movement, more powerful."

Again the mountain seemed to lift and drop, and again. Movement followed movement. All around the clatter of rocks told of stone splitting, breaking and falling. "How can this be?" Khaajd scrambled to her feet. "I've never felt the mountains move so!"

"Neither have I," Thaakumek said, "but I have heard of it. Something of the like happened some fifty years before I hatched. The whole range shook, rumbled and clattered. Cliffs collapsed. Rivers switched to new paths. Lakes vanished or appeared where no lake had been. Great cracks appeared in the rock. This is not new, Khaajd, just rare."

"Something bigger than both us and the humans," Khaajd murmured.

"It's certainly that," Thaakumek agreed. "If ever I doubt your feelings in the future just remind me of this moment and ..." She stopped dead. There was a new sound. A different sound. In the distance began a rumble that grew into an increasing roar. A roar that expanded to a crescendo, filling the night with sound and fury, before slowly, slowly fading away again. "What was that?" For the first time Khaajd heard the uncertainty of panic in the queen's voice.

"The humans' water wall!" Khaajd cried with sudden realisation. "The shaking of the mountains has broken the dam they built to contain the lake! What we heard was the fury of the water."

"And beneath the lake is the city itself," Thaakumek said. "Come, Khaajd, fly with me. Back to Yullat to see what may be seen now!"

Khaajd's weakness seemed to vanish with the moment of realisation. She practically hurled herself down the slope and into the air. With Thaakumek at her side she flew back to the vantage point she had so recently vacated. The sight that greeted them in the slowly gathering light of pre-dawn was very different to the one they had seen in the deepening darkness of the evening before. Before them stretched a vista of absolute chaos and total destruction.

The northern half of the city had taken the full force of the avalanche of water, and here almost nothing remained. Buildings, walls, towers and everything else lay shattered and scattered like so much insubstantial fluff before a howling gale. Northern Yullat had, in scant moments, simply ceased to exist as anything meaningfully resembling a city. The southern half of the city may have avoided the full force of the water, but even here buildings were crumbled and towers felled by the shaking of the mountains itself.

Everywhere was water, but not clean water. In its ferocious passage the freed lake had picked up all. Mud and scum, the filth from the sewers and the sties of pigs, everything vile and foul that fast flowing water could find had indeed been found and brought into view. Among the shattered debris floated the bodies of dead things. Rats, cats, dogs, horses, pigs and people joined each other in a macabre dance of the dead as the eddies swirled. Creatures of every kind, united only in having been in the wrong place at the wrong time.

Through the water waded people, their faces ashen, their eyes wide with horror and pain. In their arms they carried children, pets, belongings and anything else they considered of value as they desperately tried to find a path from where they were to somewhere, anywhere, less hellish. Many wore the attire of bed, many struggled and cried out from injury, and none knew where they could go or what they could do to save themselves. They just hoped somewhere else would be better than here.

A confident, sure, strong world had collapsed in seconds, leaving behind a barely recognisable ruin.

"This changes everything!" Thaakumek murmured.

"No." Khaajd's voice was both shocked and saddened. "It changes nothing at all."

The dragon queen looked at her companion, unsure if her ears had failed her. "Their walls are down. Their towers, broken. Their defences lie in shattered ruin. The city below us is doomed. Bhuul and his battle dragons could sweep in and wipe out what is left for barely the loss of a single dragon!"

"And what of that?" Khaajd asked. "Yullat would be gone, just as Tekmir is gone, but what would <u>really</u> be different? Once more dragons would have slaughtered on a massive scale humans who had already been half-crushed by something else. We would have shown how vicious we are. How brutal. How merciless and cruel, but do the humans really need another lesson in those qualities? They know already, from Tekmir." Khaajd swept her gaze across the scene in front of her. "So how much time would the slaughter of Yullat buy us, Thaakumek? Five extra years before we're all butchered? I doubt even that! The humans have reason to hate us already, but surely the cold-blooded butchery of these helpless and desperate people would fill them with such venom and hunger for retribution that they would double their efforts to crush us, not halve them. We would, once more, enjoy a short moment of savagery and slaughter. Then we would pay for our gloating as vengeance howled around us. <u>Nothing</u>

has changed here, Thaakumek. Nothing at all. Not unless <u>we</u> change, and become what we have never been before."

Thaakumek stood in silence for half a minute. When she spoke her voice was soft. "What must we become, Khaajd?"

"We must become a noble people," Khaajd replied. "We must become a people who care for <u>all</u>, and not just for ourselves. We must not kill these humans, Thaakumek, we must save them. They have seen us as enemies and learned to treat us as such. How could they not? Let them, for once, see us as friends. Who knows, they might learn that lesson too."

Thaakumek turned to look at the shattered city below. She shuffled her forefeet, a sure sign of confused indecision. "<u>Save</u> them?"

"What other option do we have?" Khaajd asked. "What other real option, I mean? Butchery has bought us nothing, Thaakumek. Butchery has always bought us nothing. It can never do anything but buy us nothing. We are a doomed people unless we can become a <u>different</u> people, and hope the humans are willing to become a different people with us."

"Will they become a different people if we do?" Thaakumek asked. "You know them, Khaajd. Tell me!"

"I don't know," Khaajd confessed, "but I know they will not if we do not. Why should they change? They're <u>winning</u>! Which would you prefer, Thaakumek? Some chance? Or none at all? The possibility of peace, or the absolute certainty of a war we can never win? You once told me there was nothing you wouldn't be willing to do to save your people, will you not take a chance and try a new approach?"

Still Thaakumek's feet shuffled. "It's hard," the dragon queen admitted. "Somehow hating and fearing humans has become … habit. It's what we've always done, and it's easier to do again what you've done in the past. To change direction you need to admit that you were going the wrong way before." She looked back at Khaajd. "Are you <u>sure</u> of this? Really sure?"

"I'm sure <u>something</u> must change."

Thaakumek looked back at the city. "I would fight until I didn't have strength to snap my jaws," she murmured. "I would fly until my wings collapsed. I would do anything to save my people. Anything. Even ..." her feet stopped shuffling "... even this. Yes, Khaajd, I'm with you! Yet what can we do? What do these people need that we can give them?"

Khaajd scanned the wading, broken humans. "It's winter and they have little shelter. Their clothing is wet and they have no fires for warmth. Their city is either crushed or flooded. Their food will be soiled, their water foul. I see men, women and children who are injured, with flowing blood and broken bone. They need medical care, but there will be little for them. They need so <u>much</u>!"

"But so much that we do not have!" Thaakumek said. "We have no human food or human clothes. We could hunt them a few goats or bring them a few tree branches for fuel, but what can that do for a hundred thousand or more? To say 'we must help these people' is one thing, but we need the means to do so."

"We do not need to find clothes, food, fuel and shelter for these people," Khaajd said. "The humans themselves have that. There are vast, lowland cities just a little away from the mountains that could supply all Yullat neads, and would willingly do so to aid the plight of these people. The problem is that those supplies would need to be brought here. How, Thaakumek? Pack ponies weaving for days through the mountains, along winding roads broken by the shaking of the ground ...?"

"Or by dragons flying <u>over</u> the mountains!" Thaakumek cried. "Each bringing more in an hour than could be transported by a dozen pack horses in a week! Yes, Khaajd. That I can see. Yet how will the humans trust us? We can hardly fly to the lowland cities, land in their fields, and call 'Can you spare some supplies for Yullat?'"

"True indeed!" agreed Khaajd. "We cannot do this alone. We need the humans with us. We need them to make available the supplies so that we can carry them. Both peoples must work together. Side by side, each in the full knowledge and understanding of what the other does. We need to talk to these people, Thaakumek. We need to convince them that we really do want to help rather than slaughter."

"Can we do that?" Thaakumek's voice sounded unsure. "Why should they trust us?"

"I don't know if they will trust us," Khaajd murmured, "we certainly have given them good reason not to, but it's the only hope they have."

Once more Thaakumek's feet shuffled. The doubt was back, even though the nature of the doubt was different. "So what will you do? Walk down to the city below and say 'Hello, I'm Khaajd. I want to save the people of Yullat'?"

Khaajd considered a moment. "Yes," she said softly. "I think that is more or less exactly what I shall do."

"Be careful, Khaajd! For all the destruction there will be ten thousand or more guardsmen down there. Guardsmen with crossbows. If they turn against you they'll cut you to pieces before you can flee."

"That is a risk I must take," Khaajd said, "but before that we must get news to Bhuul. He will have felt the mountains shake, just as we did. Not just here but elsewhere. He also might have seen towers fall."

Khaajd saw Thaakumek's eyes widen slightly in alarm. "That is a good point! We must get message to him, and fast, that no attack must be made against any humans." She lifted her head to the sky and twisted her neck, scanning the vastness above. "Where is a dragon when you need one!"

Khaajd joined her in the search. The sky seemed completely devoid of dragons. Then Thaakumek spotted a tiny, black speck. "There!" she called, pointing with her nose. "A fraction above the line of the mountain tops."

Khaajd howled a bellow with every ounce of her strength. The sound echoed between the mountains.

"Too far for that," Thaakumek urged. "Signal flame, Khaajd! Fast, and let's hope he sees us." She pointed her muzzle directly upwards and unleashed an immense plume of searing, white fire. As her breath failed so Khaajd replaced her queen's flame with her own. As Khaajd drew breath so Thaakumek, once more, flamed. Between them they managed to keep an almost continuous brilliance thundering into the rapidly diminishing darkness of morning.

The hope was to be seen quickly, for as the sun rose and the daylight grew even dragon fire would become less obvious. It was hard work, and exhausting.

"Come on!" Thaakumek gasped as she snatched a few deep lungfuls of air between one flame and the next. "See us!"

The black speck stopped tracking across the sky. It hung against the deep, morning blue, almost as if it wasn't moving at all. The dragon had turned and was flying directly towards them … or directly away.

"Has he turned this way?" Khaajd was panting for breath.

"I … I think so," Thaakumek replied and hurled flame into the air again. As the two dragons watched the speck became heavier and bolder against the blue. "Yes! He has!"

They watched as the speck took shape. First a tiny, flapping line against the blue. Then a distinct dragon. Khaajd looked intently. "Who is it?"

"No idea," Thaakumek replied, "and I don't care as long as he can carry a message."

Within a few minutes the speck had transformed into a massive battle dragon and Mhiirak landed beside them. He wing pressed, but even as he was doing so his intense, green eyes were viewing the destruction that had once been Yullat.

"I have a message for Bhuul," the queen said.

Not even his queen's voice was enough to drag Mhiirak's eyes from the city. "I can guess the nature of that message!" His voice was edged with savagery.

"You may guess," Thaakumek informed him, "but I suspect you would be wrong in that guess." Those words attracted Mhiirak's full attention! "I need to get an urgent message to Bhuul that no humans are to be attacked. Not here, not anywhere. That is my absolute command. He is to choose reliable dragons to act as messengers to spread my word through the mountains. All dragons, male and female, old and young must hear and understand. I further want him to arrange patrols through the mountains, overflying the human towns and villages, and following their roads. These patrols are to stay high so that they cause no alarm, but they must watch for any signs of aggression against the humans in breach of my command. If they see such ill-discipline they are to take whatever steps are required to halt it."

Mhiirak was stunned to near speechlessness. He could hardly believe what his ears were telling him. "We … we …" Eventually he managed to force his voice to express his shock. "… we are to protect the humans?"

"Yes," confirmed Thaakumek. "Even if that forces us to act with aggression against those of our own kind who do not have the loyalty to obey their queen's command."

There was a full minute of total silence. "Bhuul will think I have lost my mind," Mhiirak murmured.

"No," Thaakumek assured him. "He will think I have lost mine, yet I have never been more serious, Mhirrak. I am convinced the whole future of our people depends on this. We have one last chance and if we fail in it we are surely doomed."

Mhiirak's head turned from Thaakumek to Khaajd. His eyes bored into her, yet his question remained directed at his queen. "Who convinced you of this, Thaakumek?"

"I did." Khaajd accepted responsibility before her queen could reply.

"No." Thaakumek's voice was certain. "The truth convinced me. Yet I was fortunate to have with me someone who both understood, and had the courage to voice, that truth."

Mhiirak looked back and forth between the two female dragons. He took a couple of huge breaths, releasing them slowly. "I shall carry your message," he said, "though how Bhuul will react to it I do not know."

Thaakumek tongue wrapped. "Do not doubt your battle master," she said. "I most certainly do not. There is no dragon more loyal. He may be puzzled, he may be unsure, but he will do what is needed."

Mhiirak considered. "Yes. He will. Yet many dragons in the wings will see these events as a chance to inflict defeat on the humans. A chance like none they have ever seen before. Your command will put Bhuul's authority under considerable strain."

"As it will doubtless put my own under strain," Thaakumek confessed. "Yet if I may send you on your way with a thought it would be this. These events <u>are</u> a chance to inflict defeat on the humans, but if we take that chance will we ever be able to inflict it again? I doubt it. Look at the humans in the city below us, Mhiirak. They see us up here and expect us to slaughter them. Of course they do, it's what we've always done if the opportunity presented itself. The humans expect butchery. The dragons expect butchery. <u>Everyone</u> expects butchery. I've had enough of doing what is expected of me by both our peoples, particularly when I know it does no good. Khaajd has opened my eyes and I will not close them again. This time I, and my people, will do what is <u>not</u> expected of us, yet what might give us real hope."

"Those words I shall also carry to Bhuul." Mhiirak wing pressed and flew off, leaving Thaakumek and Khaajd alone at Yullat. They watched him disappear into the distance.

"Now," Khaajd murmured, "I need to walk down into the city and see if the humans will allow me to live long enough to speak to their duke."

"They'd better!" growled Thaakumek. "If they don't then Yullat is truly doomed. I'll send in every battle dragon I have to avenge you, whatever the consequences!"

"No." Khaajd's voice was soft. "If I cannot convince them, and they kill me, then I am one dead dragon. Thousands more will still live, and their only hope is peace. Real, genuine peace built on goodwill and mutual respect. I would not have my death steal that one chance away."

Thaakumek was silent for a long time. "You ask a lot, my friend," she said. "If these humans were to kill a dragon that seeks to help them it would truly make my blood boil. I would want to see them dead for their injustice!"

"Not injustice," Khaajd said. "The humans are not an unjust people, for all we dragons believe them so. Fearful, maybe, and with good cause if truth be told. Suspicious, for sure, particularly if a dragon were to walk towards them saying things they cannot believe and have never heard a dragon say before. When I walk down to them they may well not trust me. They may well kill me. Yet maybe, after killing me, they will see you <u>still</u> do not call in the battle dragons. Perhaps, then, they will come to trust <u>you</u>."

"I do not <u>want</u> trust bought at the price of your life, Khaajd!"

"Neither do I," Khaajd said. "I want trust bought at the price of my fear and apprehension, with me living long enough to enjoy the memory. I am not suicidal, Thaakumek. I believe they will listen to me, but if I am proved wrong I must die knowing that losing my life does not mean my people lose their hope."

Thaakumek looked over the city below. "I give you my word." Her voice was a whisper.

"Thank you. And now," Khaajd wing pressed. "I go to the city." She turned and headed down the slope to the ruins. As she walked she called in the human tongue. "People of Yullat! Do not attack me, I mean you no harm! I wish to speak to your duke in peace for the good of all, human and dragon."

Ahead of her she saw movement. Men, women and children saw her approaching and turned to flee as fast as their weakened states would allow, yet not all the movement was away.

Most of the city's walls and dragon towers had collapsed, and many thousands of warriors had been killed, yet thousands more remained very much alive. From every direction she could see men in the tattered, soiled, but clearly recognisable livery of the city guard. They did not flee as others fled, they moved towards her. Even in the midst of disaster they faced another threat with courage and determination. Men armoured. Men bearing crossbows. Men with faces grim and eyes hard.

159

She carried on slowly walking. "People of Yullat! Do not attack me, I mean you no harm! I wish to speak to your duke in peace for the good of all, human and dragon."

She reached the edge of the city and stopped. Already a cordon of warriors surrounded her. First a hundred, then three hundred, then six, then a thousand. A thousand crossbows aimed unerringly at her head, ready to rip her life away. "People of Yullat! Do not attack me, I mean you no harm! I wish to speak to your duke ..."

"We hear you, dragon!" A voice cut her short. "We just don't believe you!"

Standing atop a pile of broken rubble stood a soldier. A captain, Khaajd believed from his uniform, though she was not greatly knowledgeable about such matters. He stood with his hands on his hips and a glare of mistrust in his eye. All around Khaajd the rapidly growing crowd of soldiers bristled, their fingers resting on the catches that would unleash stinging death.

"I come alone ..."

"Alone?" barked the captain. "There is another dragon on the hill above us, not half a mile distant. A huge male flew off a quarter hour ago. Your concept of 'alone' differs greatly from mine, dragon."

Khaajd paused. "One dragon perches half a mile away," she conceded, "but could that dragon save me if you commanded my death? All she could do is watch me die. I am truly alone, my fate and my life rests in your hands and those of the soldiers who surround me. I will not harm you. Even if you attack me I will not fight. I will die taking none with me to the grave. Kill me if you must, but if you do you will know you killed a creature that spoke true. All I ask is for the chance to talk to your duke. To place my words before him so that he may judge their merit for himself. When I have done so I will accept whatever fate he chooses for me, and do so without regret."

The captain considered. "You talk a pretty talk, dragon. I'll give you that."

"What have you to lose?" Khaajd asked. "With every passing minute more of your soldiers come. If you commanded my death now I would die in a half minute. As more men arrive even that death would become faster and more assured, so send word to your duke and let me wait. Nothing can be lost and, perhaps, there might be something to be gained."

The captain nodded slowly. "I would be most surprised," he called, "if my lord duke was not already aware of your presence. Very well, dragon, if you will stand where you are and threaten no-one then I shall stand where I am and issue no command to attack. Should a superior officer arrive then the matter will, of course, become his to decide. Until then, while you remain peaceful, I shall not seek your harm."

"I can ask no more."

"But I can!" snapped the captain. "Remain silent!"

Time seemed to pass very slowly. Around Khaajd the ring of crossbowmen grew until it was some twenty deep, several times over what would be needed to slay one, rather small, female dragon. On top of the rubble pile the captain who had originally spoken was joined by other officers. The men engaged in earnest discussion with much nodding, frowning, gesturing and many a glance in her direction.

Finally another man arrived, but not a man dressed as a soldier. A man who appeared familiar to Khaajd. He, too, spoke earnestly and deeply with the assembled officers, then he turned to Khaajd. "My name is Farron," he called to her. "Norras Farron. I am an advisor and aid to Duke Telchar Bliss. My lord duke is currently in the north of the city, seeking to organise the effort to save our people. This work is of the greatest importance to him, and to all of us, so he will need good reason to interrupt it. Who are you, what place do you hold among dragonkind, and what is the nature of the discussion you seek with him?"

"My name is Khaajd ..."

"Is it indeed!" Farron snapped the interruption. "That name is not unknown to us. Neither is it spoken in good favour, poisoner of wells!" Khaajd saw the officers around Farron straighten. She saw the crossbowmen that surrounded her grip their weapons tighter. She saw faces drop into angry scowls and eyes burn with vengeful anger. "Understand that when we fight your battle dragons we do so as foes, but at least we also respect them as such. Your chosen method of slaughter makes you foul beyond the worst of your kind."

"Then make your decision and act upon it," Khaajd replied. "If you would command your men to slay me, do so. If not let me speak and hear what I have to say."

For at least thirty seconds Farron just stood and glared. Then his jaw tensed. "Continue."

"My queen, Thaakumek, offers the people of Yullat, and all the other human peoples of the mountains, her aid at this time of their greatest need."

Farron actually laughed. "Aid? <u>Aid</u>? Since when has a single dragon aided a single human?"

"To my knowledge not for a thousand years, if ever. I believe it is just as rare for a human to aid a dragon."

"Then why now?" roared Farron.

"<u>Because</u> we have never done it before," Khaajd replied. "Let us try something new. Perhaps it will prove habit forming."

"<u>Balls</u>!" The obscenity echoed across the broken city.

"Then why am I here?" Khaajd asked. "If what I say is balls, as you propose, then suggest an alternative reason why I would walk into a ring of crossbowmen who could end my life in twenty seconds."

"How in the name of hell should I know why you're here ..."

"By <u>asking</u> me, as you have done!" Now it was Khaajd's turn to interrupt. "And by hearing the answer that I have given! My queen seeks to aid you. With her aid there are many in this city who will live. Many who, without that aid, will die. If you do not trust my words, and I accept there is little reason why you should, then trust my queen's <u>actions</u>. Not one hour ago she sent word, to be relayed to all dragons, that the humans of the mountains were not to be harmed or molested despite their weakened state. She instructed patrols to be formed which will overfly your towns, villages and roads to ensure that command is obeyed. Patrols what will protect <u>your people</u> at <u>my queen's command</u>. Whether you listen to me or not, whether you allow me to leave this city alive or not, my queen will not and does not seek your harm. Yet give her a chance, allow her to show you in her actions the desires of her mind, and she will do you and the people of Yullat great good. I cannot make that decision for you, but if you cannot find it in your heart to accept aid freely and willingly offered, then thousands will die who should have lived."

Farron thought a moment. "So what do <u>you</u> get out of this, dragon?" he asked. "Don't tell me it's nothing, and that you offer aid out of the kindness of dragon hearts! That, too, I will not believe. Even if help <u>is</u> being offered, what is the price to be paid?"

"There is, indeed, a price ..."

"Ha!" spat Farron. "I knew as much!"

"... and a great one," Khaajd continued. "You will have to give up something dear to you. Something you have nurtured for a thousand years. You will have to give up your hatred of dragons."

"So I must stand here and say 'I will not hate' …?" Farron's voice rang with contempt.

"No," Khaajd said. "I would demand no such words of you, and even if I did they would mean nothing. You will have to give up your hatred of dragons because it would be unjust of you to hate those who saved your people, and you are not an unjust man. The compulsion will not be mine, or my queen's. It will be your own. You will give up your hatred of dragons because we will no longer be worthy of it, and <u>you</u> will know us no longer worthy of it. I ask no promise of you or your people save one, that you should be just and honourable in your own eyes. If you are that, then it will be enough."

Farron stood in silence a while. "There is no bargain demanded?" he asked. "No concession to be made? No promise on which your aid depends?"

"None. What the dragon people can do for you they will, without condition."

"And what <u>can</u> you do?" Farron asked. "I concede a dragon's strength might be useful digging the injured out of rubble, but beyond that what we need is not what you can supply. Have you tents? Have you warm clothes? Have you clean water or food beyond a few goats snatched from the mountainside?"

Khaajd almost tongue wrapped. The same question as Thaakumek had asked. The answer was, of course, also the same. "Have you those things?"

"Of course not!" Farron exploded.

"Yes you, <u>have</u>," Khaajd corrected. "You just don't have them <u>here</u>." A sudden frown crossed Farron's face. A realisation. "There are many towns and cities where tents can be found, and food, and medicaments, and picks to dig rubble, and caskets to carry fresh water, and warm clothing … and everything else you need. So how will you get it here, Farron? Pack ponies in the mountains?

Or dragons? <u>Hundreds</u> of dragons. <u>Strong</u> dragons. Flying over the mountains rather than crawling through them to deliver what your people need in hours rather than weeks or months. Yet for this we need your duke. We cannot fly to the lowland cities and expect them to hand over supplies unless we were seen to be acting with <u>his</u> <u>blessing</u> for the good of all your people."

For a long time Farron thought. "Very well, dragon. I shall send word to my duke. I am not yet convinced ..." His voice trailed off.

"But to save the people of Yullat it's worth taking the gamble?" Khaajd suggested an ending for the thought.

"Yes," Farron conceded.

"Then may I ask a personal favour?" Khaajd asked.

"Go on."

"I confess to feeling a <u>little</u> nervous with this many crossbows aimed at my head."

Farron almost grinned. "That I can understand." He called to the crossbowmen surrounding Khaajd. "Weapons <u>down</u>, gentlemen!"

All around Khaajd the crossbows dipped.

# Chapter Thirteen

Bhuul fixed Mhiirak with emerald green eyes. There was a pause. A long pause. "She said <u>what</u>?"

"We are not, under any circumstances, to attack the humans," Mhiirak repeated. "The word is to be spread to all. We are also to assemble patrols of our best and most reliable dragons to overfly the human settlements and roads to ensure the queen's command is obeyed. These patrols are to fly high to ensure they cause the humans no anxiety."

It didn't help to have Mhiirak repeat the instruction. Bhuul found it equally incomprehensible the second time. "We are <u>not</u> to attack?"

"Under no circumstances whatever."

"She's gone mad!" Bhuul snorted.

Mhiirak tongue wrapped. "Thaakumek said you might come to that conclusion."

Bhuul's eyes didn't waver. "Did she give you any indication of why? Any at all?"

"She left me with a final thought before I took off," Mhiirak replied. "She said these events are a chance to inflict defeat on the humans, but if we take that chance we may never be able to inflict it again. The humans expect butchery. The dragons expect butchery. Everyone expects butchery, but she has had enough of doing what is expected of her by both our peoples, particularly when she knows it does no good. This time she and her people will do what is not expected of them, yet might give real hope."

"And this doing <u>nothing</u> gives us real hope?"

"I don't think we will do nothing," Mhiirak said. "We just won't do what is expected."

"Well, she's managed to avoid the expected with me!" Bhuul growled. Then he tongue wrapped. "It seems I have work to undo."

"Undo?"

"For the last half day I've been flying through the mountains telling the wings to gather for attack," Bhuul said. "Within an hour's flight of where we now stand two hundred or more have already arrived, with more landing as we speak. Now I must tell them I was wrong. They will be confused, astonished … and probably not best pleased. Particularly as I cannot tell them why!"

"I will come with you," Mhiirak said, "and stand beside you as you tell them."

"No," Bhuul said. "I will tell the wings, and there will be no trouble there. Battle dragons are disciplined and loyal, that's <u>why</u> they're battle dragons. I need you to get yourself into the mountains and spread Thaakumek's command to those dragons <u>not</u> in the wings. As soon as a few of my battle dragons have recovered from the shock I'll send them out to do the same. You will not be able to talk to all, there must be fifteen thousand dragons in the mountains, but if you can get word to some and tell them to tell others, then the news will travel."

"Of course."

"Yet do another thing for me," Bhuul added. "I would trust any battle dragon I command with my life, but I would be less inclined to trust the rest! There are hate-filled fools out there who will hear the queen's command but not have the wisdom or self control to obey it. As you talk to dragons, <u>listen</u> to them as well. There will certainly be opposition to Thaakumek's … new approach. We need to find out how much opposition and how serious. Keep your eyes open, your ears open, and your wits about you. Let me know how things <u>really</u> stand among our people."

Mhiirak's head tilted. "You think there might be real trouble?"

"I think Thaakumek has <u>no idea</u> how badly this command of hers will be taken by many dragons," Bhuul replied. "Our job, yours and mine my friend, is to make sure things don't get out of control."

Mhiirak understood. "Hatred often snarls but rarely listens," he murmured. "Yes, Bhuul. I see your point. Leave the matter to me, I shall tell you how it stands … however that may be."

"Good," Bhuul rumbled. "After I have spoken to the wings I shall head for Yullat to see what Thaakumek intends. Meet us there when you have anything to tell us."

Each went their separate way, Bhuul to speak to the gathered battle dragons of the wings, and Mhiirak to speak to the ordinary dragons of the mountains. Bhuul's task was by far the quicker and, as he predicted, there was a fair amount of grumbling and snarling among dragons who had believed themselves gathering in order to attack. Yet also, again as he predicted, these same dragons accepted their queen's command and declared themselves willing to wait and watch as events unfolded. Perhaps they didn't do so with the greatest of conviction, but they did so.

It was late evening, with the light fading fast, when Bhuul arrived at Yullat to find Khaajd lounging at ease on a ridge above the city. Thaakumek was nowhere to be seen.

"She's hunting," Khaajd told him.

Bhuul looked at her. "Good. Then perhaps, in her absence, you can tell me what is happening."

"We're trying a new approach."

Bhuul considered the words. "So Mhiirak told me, and I admit the old one was was not greatly successful. Yet what new approach is there?"

"We're going to be friends rather than enemies," Khaajd said.

"For how long?" Bhuul asked.

"For ever, if it works."

Bhuul settled beside Khaajd. "That's it? The new plan in its entirety? We're going to be nice and hope they'll be nice in return?"

"More or less," Khaajd confirmed. "We're going to help the people of this city survive the disaster that has befallen them, and once we have done so we shall see if they are still as ill disposed towards us as they were before."

Bhuul could hardly have looked more unconvinced. "You believe this will work?"

"I believe what we were doing did <u>not</u> work, so this approach could hardly be less successful."

Bhuul tongue wrapped. "That is not the question I asked."

Khaajd allowed herself a few seconds to consider the expansion of her answer. "I am hopeful. Humans have a sense of honour. A sense of justice and fair play. If you do a good deed for a human they will tend to think better of you, and act better towards you."

"So we will sit on the mountain tops and do nothing but watch as the humans recover from disaster and re-build their city?"

"Oh no!" This time it was Khaajd who tongue wrapped. "We will do far more than sit and watch. We will assist them. In truth we'll probably not help them re-build as such, for all your many talents I do not see you as a layer of bricks, but we'll certainly help them survive the disaster. We will bring them the food, the clothing, the blankets, the fresh water, the picks and shovels, and everything else they need. In doing so we will save the lives of many humans. Humans who will know they would have died but for us. Humans who will tell the whole human world that a dragon as a friend is a thousand times better than a dragon as an enemy. Humans who, when they've seen what could be, will not want to go back to what was."

"But there will be many other humans," Bhuul said, "whose feelings towards us will not have changed at all."

"Of course," Khaajd conceded. "Just as there will be many a dragon who will never be able to look upon a human without loathing. It won't be easy, Bhuul, and there will be mountains of mistrust on both sides, yet what has happened here presents us with a chance, a single chance, to show that we don't have to be ravenous slaughterers. If we can show that, then many humans will begin to look on us a new way. We may not win over all the human population, but at least we will have some friends among them. Some is surely better than none at all."

Bhuul considered. "Thaakumek has agreed to this new policy?"

"She has," Khaajd confirmed, "and I have been down to the city below to talk to the humans. To a man called Farron and then to a man called Bliss. The man called Bliss is the human duke, as Thaakumek is to us so he is to them."

"You spoke as a dragon?" Bhuul asked.

"I spoke the human tongue, of course, but physically I was a dragon."

Bhuul was surprised. "They listened to you without seeking your death?"

"It was a close matter at the beginning," Khaajd admitted, "but I can hardly blame them for their suspicions. Wouldn't you have been suspicious in their place?"

"Yes," Bhuul admitted.

"However I managed to convince them that I was, at the least, worth talking to. Then we were able to discuss what really matters. When I spoke to the duke we talked in detail about what needed to be done and how we should set about doing it. He needs us to fly to the lowland cities for him, collect supplies and bring them urgently to Yullat. This afternoon and evening the air has been full of messenger pigeons, carrying the duke's word to the other cities. Telling them that dragons are offering their aid and should not be attacked if they approach in peace, seeking those desperately needed supplies."

"And these messages will be enough?" Bhuul asked. "Forgive me, Khaajd, but I will still feel wary landing and walking up to a human city, even if a small bird has carried the duke's word there!"

Again Khaajd tongue wrapped. "As would I, Bhuul," she said, "so the duke's pigeons will need to be backed by something far more substantial and certain. The duke wants his aid and advisor, Farron, to travel to the lowland cities carrying his word in person, and organising the supply of what is needed from the other end."

"So how will this man, Farron, <u>get</u> to the lowland cities?" Bhuul asked. "With the roads cracked and broken that will take many days by itself."

"Not," Khaajd replied, "if he is carried by a battle dragon. A dragon that I happen to know is greatly skilled at carrying humans in his left, front talon."

Bhuul stared at her. "You want <u>me</u> to carry this man around the human world?"

"Who better?" Khaajd replied. "The duke is sending his most trusted man, and with him travels Thaakumek's most trusted battle dragon. If you and Farron cannot speak with authority on behalf of your own peoples and their rulers, who can? Farron will acquire the supplies that are needed here, and you will arrange delivery."

Bhuul was silent a moment. "It will not be as simple as that."

"Of that I am certain," Khaajd agreed. "It will probably be little better than chaos, to start with at least. Yet once things start to happen we'll have a fighting chance to impose some order on the chaos, yet most important of all is you, Bhuul. Are you willing to try and make this work?"

"If that is the role Thaakumek has chosen for be," Bhuul answered, somewhat gruffly, "then that is the role I shall fulfil as best I can."

"Neither Thaakumek nor I can think of anyone we would rather choose or place our trust in."

A deep rumble emanated from Bhuul's throat. "So where do we start?"

"I'll take you down to the city and introduce you to Farron," Khaajd said. "Come on, Bhuul, before Thaakumek gets back with my goats!"

# Chapter Fourteen

"Clear those landing areas! Fast!" Khaajd's voice echoed from the ridge above. "Come on! We have four ... no, <u>five</u> dragons waiting to land!

The duke looked up at the sound and then turned a Torm who stood beside him There was a smile on his lips. "She's quite a task mistress, that one," he observed.

"She's <u>the</u> task mistress," Torm replied. "You may have appointed Captain Rosney as commander here, but in truth Khaajd commands. Men, dragons <u>and Rosney</u> all jump when she bellows."

The duke nodded. "So how does it go here?"

"The truth?" Torm grinned. "It's chaos, but improving. Two days ago it was <u>total</u> chaos, now it's only <u>partial</u> chaos."

"The main problems?"

"Lack of communication coupled with over enthusiasm," Torm said. "The lowland cities know we're in desperate need, and want to aid us in every way they can. So when a dragon arrives, and they don't happen to have what we've asked for, they load the beast up with anything else they feel might be useful and send him back. As a result practically every available pick, shovel and wheelbarrow in the known world suddenly ended up here. We've also got a small mountain of coiled rope, paraffin camping stoves coming out of our ears, and even a couple of small, flat-bottomed river boats from Panalis that they hoped would be 'of use in the floods'."

"Good God," the duke muttered.

"Thankfully that problem seems to be reducing. The queen's battle dragon, Bhuul, has been flying Farron around the lowland cities. He's been telling them, quite forcefully I understand, that if we don't ask for something it's because we don't damn well want it. Perhaps the message is sinking in."

"Good," the duke said. "But other than that we're getting what we need without serious problem?"

Torm's smile faded. "Except for three men dead and a forth to join them before long."

"Dear God! What happened?"

"Their own damn stupid fault," Torm said, "but no less tragic for that. They were clearing 'yellow' landing area ..."

"Yellow?"

"... We have four landing areas for the dragons," Torm explained. "Each is marked out with little flags of a particular colour. Yellow, red, green and blue."

The duke nodded. "Ah! Of course."

"Well," Torm continued, "they cleared 'yellow' and shouted to Khaajd that they were out of the way so the next dragon could land. Khaajd called in the next dragon, and it was then that they realised they'd left something in the landing area. Instead of alerting Khaajd and admitting they'd fucked up, they tried to dash in and grab it before the dragon arrived. They didn't make it and he came down right on top of them. Three dead, literally smeared over the mountainside like so much mush, and the forth so badly crushed it's a miracle he lived to see this morning. He certainly won't see the next."

The duke ran his hands through his hair. "Well, you can't blame the dragon for that."

"Certainly not," Torm agreed. "He had no idea they were there at all until he was practically dropping on top of them. By then it was way too late."

"Damn! Damn! Damn! So have the procedures been tightened?"

"Let's say the lesson has been well learned," Torm replied. "You never keep anything from Khaajd, however stupid it will make you look."

The duke nodded. "Better to look a fool than to look like purée, though I suspect there will always be dangers when two hundred pound humans work closely with two hundred ton dragons."

"Indeed there will."

The duke sighed. "So other than this ... misfortune ... how has it been working with Khaajd?"

"She's worth her weight in gold."

The duke glanced up at the dragon on the ridge above them. "That's a lot of weight," he observed.

"And a lot of worth," Torm added. "She's been up there for two days and two nights without sleep, overseeing the work. The dragon queen hunts her goats that she bolts down in the lulls, and she has disappeared a few times for a handful of minutes each. I haven't asked, but I guess even a dragon hears the call of nature on occasion."

"And hopefully gets her muzzle into a clean river and drinks her fill while she's at it," the duke murmured. "Yet at some point even a dragon will need to sleep."

"And at that time some other dragon will have to take over this work," Torm said. "I assume the dragons themselves are considering that. It's for them to arrange rather than us. So, my lord, leaving dragons aside how fares the city?"

The duke considered his words with care. "It's bad," he said, "but in truth it would have been much worse but for the supplies the dragons bring in to us. We have thousands of dead and missing. Men, women and children buried under collapsed buildings. People drowned, crushed, frozen to death, poisoned through drinking foul water and killed by injuries that would have been treatable had we had the supplies to treat them. Then we have thousands more who are currently freezing and starving, without warm clothes or shelter. Yet, on the bonus side, many others will spend tonight in a tent, with good food and water inside them, warm and safe, for the first time since the disaster, and the number of these lucky souls grows with every passing hour."

Torm nodded. "Largely due to the dragons."

"Almost entirely due to the dragons," the duke corrected. "In the last two days we have received only two caravans of supplies by road, a total of sixteen pack horses. In the absence of the dragons that's all we would have received. Practically nothing. The dragons are the only hope this city has, and will remain the only hope for weeks or even months to come."

"Which will place us very much in debt to our new-found friends."

"It will certainly mean they deserve a great deal better from us than they have received in the past," the duke murmured.

"Does that bother you, my lord?"

The duke considered. "In a way, yes. It bothers me. A time will come when I have to speak to the queen of dragons knowing how much I and my people owe her and hers. When that time comes I shall either have to prove myself as worthy, or forever hang my head in shame."

"And proving yourself as worthy will be hard?" Torm asked.

"It will mean admitting faults that, perhaps, I'd rather not admit to," said the duke. "And making concessions that, while just, will be difficult to make."

"It's easier being an enemy than a friend?"

"It's certainly a damn sight <u>simpler</u>," the duke said. "To be an enemy you only have to be vicious, uncaring and filled with self-interest. To be a friend you have to be just and fair ..." He looked thoughtful a moment. "... Yet that is for the future. The only thing that matters for now is saving lives, and to save them we need the dragons. Let's not forget that they offered us help <u>in advance</u>, with no price save that we should do what we ourselves believe is right and noble."

"That might prove a very cunning position," noted Torm.

"You're damn right it is!" The duke actually grinned. "Had they demanded specific concessions then we would have debated them, agreed to those we could, and that would have been it. Debt paid in full. End of story, and everything back to normal with a clear conscience. By demanding nothing from us but our honour we are forced to do what <u>we</u> believe is right, and that forces us to think about what actually <u>is</u> right."

"And what we have been doing in the past that <u>isn't</u>," Torm added.

"Exactly."

"And that's a bad thing?" Torm asked.

"No," the duke admitted wryly. "It's not a bad thing, but there will be instances where the truth is inconvenient and in the past we've managed to avoid it. That will have to change and many will not want it to."

"The mining concerns in the mountains?"

"Them and others," the duke replied.

From the ridge above came human voices, calling loudly but still vastly lighter in tone than Khaajd's great bellows. "Red clear!" and "Green clear!"

"At last!" Khaajd's voice roared in reply, then she switched to the rumble of dragon speech and pointed her nose to the sky above.

"What does she say?" the duke hissed to Torm.

"Who's next? ..." Torm translated as Khaajd called. "... Next two! ... Ah! Shiikanat and ... and who? ... Phuuris ... Good ... Shiikanat to red ... No! Red you deaf worm! ... Phuuris to green ... Watch me, both of you. If I send up signal flame there's a problem and you must not land if there's any way you can avoid it." Torm grinned at the duke. "She says that every time now, since those men were killed. She watches the landing areas and will flame if she sees anything on them."

"Good for her," murmured the duke.

The two men watched as two dragons split away from the circling group above and swept away from the city, losing height as they went. Perhaps ten miles out they turned and lined up for the landing areas. Of course neither Torm nor the duke could recognise Phuuris or Shiikanat by sight, so it was only when they were heading back in to land that they could see which dragon was which.

A man in uniform appeared beside them. It was Captain Rosney, the soldier supposedly 'in charge'. He had papers in his hand to which he referred. "Phuuris," he muttered. "Let's see. Ah yes, Phuuris went to Nalkolah to collect a new water bowser they've made for us. Shiikanat went to Panalis for, what was it? Ah! Grain and vegetables. Excellent!"

As the dragons approached they could see what they carried. One held in his fore-claws a large, rough hewn pole. From this hung what appeared to be a gigantic barrel. The other carried a vast, brown, leather reinforced sack about the size of half a dozen horses. It bulged with goods. As they approached and cupped their wings they swung their hips far under them so that they could land on their rear feet and lower their goods gently to the ground. Barely had they landed, though, before Khaajd was bellowing again.

"Phuuris! Shiikanat! ..." Again Torm translated. "... Back into the air, fast, so the humans can clear these things away ... Hunt, drink, sleep if you must, then back here and I'll tell you where you go next." The two dragons hurled themselves into the air and Khaajd reverted to the human tongue. "Clear red and green! Come on! We haven't got all day!"

"And so it continues," Torm said. "Day and night. Now workmen will rush into those two landing areas and clear away what the dragons have brought us so the next dragons can land. It gets carried down here by other teams of men with mules, or winches and pulleys if it happens to be a single large item like the bowser. Down here it gets sorted and sent to where it's needed."

"Do we need more landing areas?" the duke asked.

"We're making up the marker flags for black and white as we speak," Torm said. "That will be six, but it still might not be enough. There's talk of the dragons arranging another complete set of landing areas further along the valley.

The duke nodded. "Excellent work. Well now I have to go and see what happens to these supplies once we get them. I will bid you good day, gentlemen."

Torm grasped his hand and Rosney saluted.

A day later, and Khaajd was showing obvious signs of exhaustion. It had now been three full days since she had slept and Thaakumek could see the dullness in her eyes and the weariness in her body. Every time a dragon landed the queen saw Khaajd's head dip with weakness, and each time it seemed to take more effort to raise it again to call in the next dragon. Someone else had to take over, and soon.

Thaakumek would have done so herself. True, her command of the human tongue wasn't a match for Khaajd's but it was adequate for this task. It was Khaajd, herself, who had argued against it saying Thaakumek should not get involved in the everyday bustle and work of the relief effort. A queen should act like a queen, particularly in front of the humans.

Still, as Thaakumek watched the fading Khaajd, there would soon be no choice unless another option presented itself. Khaajd had to rest before she made a mistake. At least she had been eating well. Every day Thaakumek had brought her five goats, and every day all five had been consumed. A good sign.

"Thaakumek!" A faint and distant dragon voice called.

She lifted her head and swivelled it, searching for the source of the call. There, in the distance, was the rapidly enlarging shape of a dragon. She tilted her head in an effort to recognise who it was, not that there would be any difficulty just a few seconds later as the dragon approached.

It turned out to be Mhiirak, and within a minute she felt the gale of his wings flow over her as he cupped them to land at her side. He wing pressed and spoke without waiting. "Thaakumek, we need to talk."

Thaakumek was puzzled. "Then talk," she suggested.

Mhiirak looked around. "Not here," he said. "There is at least one human in this city who can understand our tongue. What I have to say is not for human ears."

That sounded ominous. Thaakumek glanced across at Khaajd and called. "Mhiirak wants to speak with me a while. Will you be alright?"

"Of course," came the reply.

Thaakumek could hear the dullness in her voice to match the dullness in her eyes. She turned back to Mhiirak. "She needs to rest."

"Then when we have spoken I shall return and learn from her what must be done," Mhiirak promised. "When she is satisfied I can serve the purpose I will take over so that she can sleep. That, however, must come later. My words are urgent."

For a moment Thaakumek hesitated, wondering what needed to be said with such urgency. Then she made up her mind. "Follow me," she said and took off. They flew only a short distance, just a few miles to ensure no prying human ear would hear, then they landed. "So what needs to be said, Mhiirak?"

Mhiirak shuffled uncomfortably. "I was given a task by Bhuul. I was to carry word of your command about not attacking humans around the mountains. Bhuul, himself, would tell the battle wings, but I was to spread the word among the dragons who were not in the battle wings. The ordinary dragons of the mountains."

That didn't sound like a task that would generate a need for discrete discussion, but there was something in Mhiirak's voice that suggested something more sinister. "And …?"

"And Bhuul also asked me to listen to the ordinary dragons."

Thaakumek's head tilted a fraction. "He thought there might be a special need for this?"

Mhiirak collected his thoughts. "Bhuul believed that the battle wings had the discipline to set aside their hatred of the human race and obey your command, but he felt less sure about the rest of dragonkind. He feared … opposition. Strong opposition. Maybe even defiance and ..." Mhiirak fell silent.

"And rebellion?" Thaakumek asked softly.

"He did not use that word," Mhiirak said, "but that is how I heard his concern. So, as commanded, I flew and talked and listened. The more I listened the more I realised Bhuul's fears were well grounded. I heard dragons expressing views that were shameful. Views no dragon should ever express. Foul opinions and vile accusations."

Thaakumek's head dipped. "Tell me."

"It would be inappropriate ..."

"How can I face the truth if I do not know what is being said!" Thaakumek snapped. "Tell me!"

Mhiirak took a deep breath. "There is a strong and widespread belief that your new policy of co-operation with the humans is nothing more than craven surrender. That you have sold yourself to the human duke, preferring to live as his pet and plaything than die as a queen of dragons. That you have betrayed your people and condemned them all. There is steadily growing talk of defiance against your will and command. Of rebellion or even widespread, full scale revolt. Many who oppose you whisper their treachery in every ear foolish enough to listen, and as their whispers go unchallenged they get bolder and louder."

"Then we must speak the other view!" Thaakumek said. "We must tell our people the truth!"

"With whom?" Mhiirak asked. "Your strength is the battle wings. They are loyal to you and believe in you, but half of them are flying patrols protecting the humans and the other half are flying supplies into Yullat! Which of those are you prepared to <u>not do</u>, in order to have battle dragons free to quell the growing revolt in the mountains?"

"But we must still do both of those things!" Thaakumek was horrified. "If dragonkind will not obey my command then it's only the patrols that are keeping the humans safe from attack, and at Yullat our efforts are just beginning to win the support and trust of the duke! We can't just <u>stop</u>. It would, at a stroke, destroy all that we have just begun to build. We <u>must</u> keep the patrols flying, <u>and</u> keep aiding Yullat. We have no choice."

"Then we have <u>no battle dragons</u> that are free to send into the mountains and restore your command and authority."

Thaakumek's head dipped in despair. Her muzzle hung just inches above the rock. "And I thought all was going well," she murmured. "Our <u>one chance</u>! Of peace. Of security. Of continued life and existence. Our <u>own people</u> are going to destroy it all!"

Mhiirak looked at her. "I wish I had some advice to give," he murmured.

"I wish <u>anyone</u> had some advice to give," Thaakumek replied. "I need someone else's inspiration, Mhiirak, because I have none of my own."

Mhiirak considered a moment. "Talk to Khaajd."

"What can she do?" Thaakumek asked.

"Maybe nothing," Mhiirak replied. "But one thing is for sure, if she's not told there's a problem then she <u>definitely</u> can't do anything."

"She is exhausted to the point of dropping," Thaakumek said, "and weak from malnourishment. She must eat and sleep <u>first</u>. She's in no condition for me to pile extra worries onto her before she's had a chance to recover."

185

"Then let us hope," Mhiirak said, "that by the time she has eaten and slept and recovered it is not already too late."

"If it's too late then it's too late," Thaakumek said firmly. "We have already demanded far more of Khaajd than we had any right to demand, and hurt her more than we had any right to hurt. She will sleep and eat then, once more, I shall ask her to find a way to do what no other dragon can do. If, as before, she manages to make the impossible possible then she will live the rest of her days basking in my undying gratitude."

"And those of her people," Mhiirak added. "Even those who are unworthy of her efforts."

Mhiirak saw Thaakumek's chest expand as she took a huge breath. Then, turning her head, she unleashed a howling blast of blue, killing flame at the stone of the mountainside. Moss withered. Coarse, mountain bushes flared and burned.

"Did that help?" Mhiirak asked.

"Not greatly," the queen admitted, "but sometimes it feels good to vent your frustration by flaming something, even if it's just rock."

Our people have never been easy to rule," Mhiirak observed.

"True," Thaakumek agreed, "but I didn't think we were suicidal. If we throw away our chance of friendship with the humans we die. Slowly, for sure, but certainly. In my stupidity I thought that would be as clear to other dragons as it has become to myself. Come, Mhiirak, let us return to Yullat and Khaajd. The sooner you take her work from her the sooner she is rested and I can tell her we need another miracle from her."

Mhiirak watched as Thaakumek spread her wings and launched herself into the air. "Let us hope miracles are not too rare," he murmured for his own ears only, and spread his wings to follow.

# Chapter Fifteen

A tiny predator circled and gained height, his little wings flapping furiously and his brilliant, green eyes glittering as he scanned the ground below. A hatchling not long out of the egg, only seven feet in length but already a perfect, miniature dragon. Below him stretched one of the mountain valleys, but this one was both wide enough and flat enough at the bottom to have gathered a covering of soil. It was one of the few places deep in the mountains where extensive grassland could be found.

And where there is grass there are bound to be rabbits.

From the side of the valley other brilliant, green eyes watched his climb. "Do you think he'll do it?" Thaakumek asked.

Khaajd, lying beside her queen, also watched the tiny dragon. "He's climbing high. It looks like a steep, fast stoop to me. Hit the ground with a good, hard thump and hope the rabbit freezes a moment, long enough for him to grab it before it runs."

The queen rumbled in agreement. "That's what I'd do in his place."

"But not what I'd do," observed Khaajd.

Thaakumek looked at her. "You'd come in low and slow? Try to snatch one on the way through?"

"No." Khaajd tongue wrapped. "I'd come in low and <u>fast</u>, flaming them on the way through. Then I'd turn around, land, and spend the next five minutes picking dead rabbits out of the charred grass."

Thaakumek also tongue wrapped. "That wouldn't teach you much by way of hunting skills."

"No," Khaajd admitted, "but I'd end up with my belly full of rabbit."

The queen watched intently. "Let's hope this hatchling is more conventional in his approach. Ah! He's stopped climbing, now he circles looking for a suitable rabbit."

The speck of a hatchling was sweeping in wider arcs now, his nose pointing at the ground bellow and his wing beats less vigorous. "What do you reckon his chances are?" Khaajd asked.

The queen considered. "Not good, I'd say. Rabbits are small, agile and very fast. One in three, maybe one in four. Were you brought here to learn to hunt?"

Khaajd's eyes remained fixed on the small, circling dragon. "No. Not here but another valley way off to the south west."

Thaakumek glanced at her. "A bit narrower than this one? Curved along its length?"

"Yes."

The queen's eyes returned to the hatchling above. "I know the one. Ah! There he goes ... Nice stoop, well cupped wings ... Good control ... Down ... Down ... <u>Now</u>! ... Grab it! Grab it! ... <u>No</u>! ... Too slow." In the valley below the little dragon whirled and snapped as rabbits scattered in all directions. Within seconds there was not a rabbit to be seen anywhere.

He lifted his head and a high-pitched whine of frustration wafted to the ears of the listening dragons. "It's no use complaining about it," Khaajd murmured too softly to carry to the hatchling. "You were just too slow."

"He'll get better," the queen said. "This time he missed, and the next time he may do the same, but sometime soon he'll get it right and get his rabbit. I would guess before the sun sets this evening."

The hatchling snapped at a few dandelions in peeved frustration, he then threw himself into the air and flapped his way across to the other side of the valley. There, waiting for him, was the huge shape of an adult female and the much smaller shapes of four clutch siblings. Mother and young waited for the rabbits to return so the next of the brood could try their luck.

Thaakumek appeared to steel herself. "Khaajd, I have a problem."

Khaajd glanced at her. "I guessed as much. You had Mhiirak take over from me at the landing areas ..."

"Which I would have done anyway," Thaakumek interrupted. "You were practically collapsing on the hillside. Indeed I should have made that arrangement some time ago, you're not a strong dragon."

"True," Khaajd admitted, "but then after I'd slept you asked me to fly here with you, well away from prying ears. Besides which I know you well enough to see when you're not at ease, even when you seek to hide it."

Thaakumek considered a moment. "I had hoped it was not that obvious."

"It wasn't," Khaajd reassured her. "Or not, at least, to most dragons. What is the problem and how can I assist you?"

"I can tell you the problem, but how you can help is another matter. I'm not even sure you can."

"Then let us start with what is known," Khaajd said. "The problem."

"There is ... opposition ... to my new policy towards the humans."

Khaajd considered. "That I expected. There will always be a few who believe the only acceptable human is a corpse, and will oppose any policy that stops humans becoming corpses."

"If only it were a few," Thaakumek replied. "Yet Mhiirak has been flying in the mountains and talking to the dragons. There is great resentment. Many believe themselves betrayed ..."

"Betrayed?" Khaajd snapped. "Nonsense!"

"Nonsense indeed," Thaakumek agreed, "but such views are still voiced, and louder with every passing day. I am, by the account of many ..." She paused, finding the words hard to say. "... a human pet. A coward queen who has sold her honour because she would rather live as a human play thing than fight and die as the queen of dragons. A betrayer of her people and unfit to rule them."

She watched anger flare in Khaajd's eyes. She watched as her friend deliberately fought her fury under control. She watched as Khaajd took a deep breath so that she could speak calmly. Even so there was an edge in the voice that replied to her. "Such views are a disgrace to any dragon."

"Mhiirak said as much."

"Mhiirak is right!" For a moment the calm vanished and Khaajd's anger echoed. Then, once more, she brought herself under control. "How serious is this?"

"Very," Thaakumek replied. "The problem is that those who support me, the battle dragons, are busy either patrolling or flying supplies into Yullat. This means that those who oppose me can speak their poison openly and without contradiction. Mhiirak is afraid of growing, full scale revolt. Deeply afraid."

There was a long pause. "You are called unfit to rule? Absurd. The problem is the other way around. Those fools don't deserve a queen like you. They are unfit to be ruled. Damn them!"

"Yet I am their queen," Thaakumek said, "and it's my duty to my people to rule them, even if there are times I would prefer to just fly into the mountains and leave them wallowing in blood until they're all dead. Yet what can I do? What options do I have? I cannot send my battle wings into the mountains to take control without withdrawing them from Yullat or the patrols, yet if I do that humans will either starve or be attacked and the last hope of peace is gone."

"So what do you want me to do?"

"I have no idea." Thaakumek's voice sounded both desperate and hopeless. "What can you do? I can think of nothing, but in the absence of other options I wanted to speak to you in the hope you could work some miracle."

"Cold blooded mass murder I do rather well," Khaajd murmured, "but miracles are not my greatest strength. Yet, perhaps …?" She stopped, mid thought.

"Perhaps …?" Thaakumek prompted.

"Maybe the humans could do something."

Thaakumek's head twisted to view her. "The humans? What can they do? They're too busy trying to stay alive to do anything for us, and even if they weren't so preoccupied how can they influence our people when I cannot?"

"I don't know," Khaajd said. "Not until I ask them ..." She met her queen's eyes. "... How much do you trust me, Thaakumek?"

That came as a complete surprise. Thaakumek found herself hesitating a moment, not at the reply but at the nature of the question. "I trust you completely. Without limit or question. Why?"

"I will go to the human duke and speak with him," Khaajd declared. "The humans can give us the one thing that would flame away your opponent's words. They can give us peace as equals. If we can persuade them to do that then the argument is won. Not a single dragon could continue to claim war is better than what their queen had won for them. Yet if I am to have a chance I must be able to negotiate and make deals. For that I must have your support and confidence, because I cannot keep flying back to you to confirm. You will need to trust me."

Thaakumek held Khaajd's eyes. "I trust you." Her voice was absolute, without doubt or reservation. "Speak to the duke, and when you speak you do so with my voice. When you bargain you do so with my full support and all my hopes. Whatever you agree is also agreed by me, with no limit or exception."

"Thank you," Khaajd murmured, "and in return I make you this promise. With every fibre of my being I shall try to find your miracle for you."

Thaakumek reached out her neck and nuzzled Khaajd's ear. "From you I would expect no less, my friend." She turned again to look across the valley at the mother and her hatchlings. "Ah! The rabbits are back above ground and another young one will try their luck!"

Khaajd also looked, a tiny speck was already climbing away from the opposite ridge. "A female this time. I wonder if she will have better fortune than her brother."

"Let us see," Thaakumek murmured as the speck circled and climbed. "Ah! She tries the same approach."

"Maybe she saw her brother's hesitation when he hit the ground and has learned from it."

"We can hope." Thaakumek flicked a glance back to Khaajd. "Tell me, what would the humans think if they saw what we now see?"

Khaajd considered. "I think they would be fascinated. They would see and respect the parallels in their own lives. Human parents teach their children the skills of life just as this dragon mother does."

"They start teaching them as soon as they're hatched?"

Khaajd tongue wrapped. "Not hatched, Thaakumek," she corrected. "Human young are born without shells."

"Like goats?" Thaakumek was astonished.

"Almost exactly like goats," Khaajd confirmed.

The queen pondered this a moment. "You know, that is something I'd never even considered," she confessed, "but now that you say it, it seems to make sense. They are more like goats then like us. Warm and fur covered, even if only on their heads. Many in number and gregarious in nature."

Khaajd tongue wrapped. "I'm sure they would be delighted to know they compare so closely!"

By now the hunter of rabbits had reached her desired height. Like her brother before her she circled, peering down to select her chosen lapin victim.

"Go on, little one," Thaakumek murmured. "I'm not one to assume that one success leads to another, but somehow it would give me hope to see you catch your rabbit for us."

Both dragon heads dipped as the hatchling stooped.

"Go on! … Go on!" Khaajd urged. "Now, grab it! … Yes!"

Both Thaakumek and Khaajd pointed their noses at the sky above and unleashed a blast of signal flame in celebration. Below them, in the grass, the female hatchling purred with delight as she bolted down her prize.

# Chapter Sixteen

A large fire burned. Over the fire, hanging from a steel tripod, was a large pot. In the pot boiled porridge. Not greatly appetising porridge, it had to be admitted, but that wasn't the point. It was hot and nourishing. In front of the pot was a line of ragged people, their clothes filthy and their eyes dull, for whom this meagre meal would mean the difference between trying to sleep half starved and merely trying to sleep hungry.

From a little way away the duke watched, a captain of guard at his side. "How are things going?" he asked.

The captain considered. "Not good," he said, "but getting better, my lord. At the start we really struggled. Not only did it take the dragons time to get up to speed with their deliveries, we also had a lot of one-offs. Tents, clothing, water bowsers, medical supplies and the like. As a result food was <u>really</u> short. Now the dragons <u>are</u> up to speed, and we already have the tents and so on, so they can bring us a lot more food. We still can't give these people as much as they'd like, and what we give them is a bit rough, but at least they're not going to starve."

"So the danger is basically over?"

"Over, my lord?" the man mused. "I wouldn't say that. In truth I wouldn't even claim it was close. We have thousands of cold, hungry, injured, weak people camped out in winter and surrounded by foul water and filth. There is a real chance of disease running rampant, and even if we avoid that fate many of the weak will still succumb. We have a true disaster, but where I believed it would kill nearly all I now think we might save three of every four."

It's strange how 'good news' was now defined as 'only' a quarter of the people dying. Disaster truly does change the perception.

"My lord duke!"

A distant call made the duke turn and scan the scene behind him. Among the broken buildings he saw the figure of a soldier scrambling towards him. The duke watched as he edged through the wreckage of the city to join them.

"My lord duke," the man repeated. "I have a message from the dragon landings. That thin female dragon, the poisoner ..."

The duke's eyes narrowed slightly. "Her name is Khaajd."

The man hesitated. "Yes, my lord, that one. She wants to speak with you. She says the matter is urgent."

"Urgent?" the duke asked. "Did she say what form the urgency took?"

"Not to my knowledge," the soldier replied. "She didn't speak to me directly. She spoke to the dragon lover."

"And his name," the duke murmured, "is Torm."

"Indeed, my lord."

The duke observed the man a while. "Have you a particular issue regarding Khaajd and Torm that makes their names distasteful to you, soldier?"

The man's eyes narrowed. "I have, or rather had, a sister in Tekmir my lord, who would still me alive if Khaajd ..." He spoke the name with strangely soft venom. "... had not poisoned the wells or if Torm ..." The same tone again. "... had alerted Tekmir to the danger she represented when he first knew of it."

The duke's jaw tensed, yet how could he criticise such feelings when a man had lost someone he loved? In this man's place wouldn't he also feel ... difficulty ... with both Khaajd and Torm? Hatred would run deep in many places, and no quick fix of assistance at Yullat would remove it from all hearts. "Yet now the dragons are the difference between life and death for the people of Yullat," he observed.

"Indeed, my lord." The man's voice reeked of mistrust. "I just wonder why they have chosen to help us. Out of the kindness of their dragon hearts? No, my lord. They want something in return."

The duke nodded. "They doubtless want many things. Wanting something is not, in itself, a crime. Let's see what this particular dragon wants on this particular occasion, and see it it's a just request."

For a moment the soldier hesitated, then he lead the way. They scrambled slowly through the wreckage of the city towards the northern ridge. There, by the landing areas, stood Mhiirak in his newly acquired role of controller of landing dragons. They did not, however, head towards him but instead made for another part of the ridge a little further along. There both men could see Khaajd, perched and waiting.

As they approached the soldier asked to be excused. He had no desire to walk closer than he needed to any living dragon. The duke went on alone. As he approached Khaajd turned to him and called. "My lord duke. It's good to see you again."

The duke had to walk a further hundred yards before his lighter voice would carry. "And good to see you, Khaajd, yet your message says you have a matter of urgency to discuss with me?"

Khaajd looked at the tiny figure, assessing him. "I have, but not one I would discuss within hearing of others. Will you allow me to carry you a little way away, where we can talk in private?"

The duke considered and grinned. "A ride in a dragon's talon? I must confess I have somewhat envied Farron that experience."

"It is little to envy." Khaajd tongue wrapped. "I know this personally, yet it would only be a few beats of the wing anyway. Half a mile or so." She stretched out a tubed talon.

"Then I shall enjoy those few beats," the duke laughed as he climbed onto her fingers. It was indeed brief. Just a minute in the air if that, before Khaajd landed and the duke once more stood with his feet on solid rock. "Different," he said.

"But not greatly comfortable." Khaajd noted.

"I confess I would choose a horse in preference," the duke admitted, "but enough of banter, Khaajd. You have a matter of importance."

Khaajd considered her words. "There is, my lord, opposition among dragonkind to Thaakumek's new policy."

"The policy of helping humans rather than killing them?" the duke said. "That does not surprise me, I fear. There is even opposition to her policy among my own people, and we're the ones being helped."

"Our problem is that Thaakumek was unaware of how strong that opposition is."

"Ah." The duke frowned. "That does not sound good. I assume she has <u>become</u> aware, and that the opposition is serious and mounting with time?"

"Many among her own people feel betrayed," Khaajd said. "They declare her unfit to rule. They name her a coward who has sold herself to humanity because she would rather live a human pet than rule as ..."

"A human pet?" The duke almost spluttered in his outrage. "A <u>human pet</u>? Your queen? That is outrageous! I have only recently come to know her, but already I see she is a creature of courage and honour. Such lies are disgusting. If I were a dragon I would be <u>ashamed</u> to hear my queen debased so!"

"I <u>am</u> a dragon," Khaajd murmured, "and I <u>am</u> so ashamed, yet my people are divided. Some part, but by no means most, truly and sincerely believe in what Thaakumek tries to do here. Perhaps a similar number are implacably opposed, and always will be. Between the two are dragons unsure, prepared to wait and see with hope in their hearts, but as yet unconvinced. The problem is that those who oppose are poisoning the views of those who remain undecided. Time passes and talk of our 'traitor queen' spreads unanswered, because we haven't the dragons to fly into the mountains and oppose it. Those dragons loyal to the queen are busy, both here and on patrol to protect your people. Those who are not loyal have the time and opportunity to talk and be heard. Thaakumek has nothing with which to counter the threat. She is losing her authority and mass rebellion looms in the mountains. Civil war, dragon against dragon."

The duke was certainly sharp enough to understand the implications. He chose a rock, sat and rested his chin on a balled fist in thought. "There are those among my people who would welcome such an outcome, fools that they are!" he murmured. "Yet in recent history only one dragon queen has sought to be a friend rather than a foe. If we lose her it would be a disaster! A chance of peace and goodwill thoughtlessly discarded that we would never get again. If we meekly sit back and let this happen the next ten generations will speak our names as curses, and rightly so! Damnation, Khaajd, I didn't <u>realise</u>. I just didn't know!"

"Why should you know?" Khaajd asked. "You have no contact whatever with dragons save the contact you have here, with us. How could you know unless we told you?"

Yet the duke was not a man to accept an easy excuse. "No, no, Khaajd, that won't do. I should have wondered. I should have asked myself the question at least. The queen of dragons offers us aid and friendship when we would have expected slaughter and fury, and it never occurred to me to question how her own people might see this gesture?"

"You have had other matters on your mind of late, my lord." Khaajd offered him a second excuse.

Like the first it was rejected. "Not so much that it should have dulled my wits! I consider myself a thoughtful man and I have proved less than that." He looked up at Khaajd. "So what do we do?"

"<u>I'm</u> going to talk to <u>you</u>," Khaajd said. "What are <u>you</u> going to do?"

The duke's chin lifted off his fist. "Me? I'm not sure what options I have."

"My queen has placed her neck in the jaws of fate for you and your people, but also for her and hers," Khaajd said. "She is wagering <u>everything</u>, her authority, her hopes and her people's lives, on this one dream of peace between human and dragon. Now that she has dreamed that dream she will not surrender it. I know her! Not <u>ever</u>. She will either make that dream true or she will die trying. There is no compromise now, no going back to what was. The question is whether you also share that dream, my lord. Are you prepared to fight for it as she will fight for it, hazarding all you have? Will you place your neck beside my queen's in the jaws of fate?"

"Ouch!" The duke's face formed both grimace and grin at the same time. "That doesn't sound greatly pleasant."

"It won't be," Khaajd admitted, "yet so far you have been most fortunate. Disaster befell Yullat and you managed to persuade the dragon race to help your people rather than killing them ..."

"I cannot claim any credit for that!" the duke objected.

Khaajd tongue wrapped. "Claim all the credit you can, my lord duke, and from everywhere you can. The time may come when you'll need all you can get. Your agreement with Thaakumek has already saved the lives of many thousands, and will save the lives of many thousands more if it, and she, survives. People sleep in tents, wrapped in warm blankets and with food in their bellies. People who would be freezing and starving were it not for what you have achieved here. You have a surplus of popularity, my lord. A surplus you can afford to hazard. Thaakumek has none."

The duke nodded slowly. "So you believe now is the time to hazard the popularity I have recently acquired?"

"Now is the time for you to lose some so that Thaakumek can gain it."

Again the duke nodded. "The dragons need to see something. They need to understand that it's not all dragons giving and humans taking, but that they get something concrete in return. Yet what?"

"The mountains."

The duke's eyes widened. "Now that is a big ask."

"Is it?" Khaajd asked. "Do you want to be a friend of dragons, or just a man who pretends to be?"

The duke looked into her burning, green eyes. "A friend," he murmured.

201

"A friend does not steal his friend's home. A friend does not condemn his friend's children to slow starvation."

For a full minute the duke remained silent. "Yet isn't there a place for <u>both</u> human and dragon in the mountains?"

"Not when one people's use of the mountains is ever expanding, and destroys them for the other. There can be no sharing with a people who will always seek to take all."

"Yet there are great resources in the mountains," the duke said.

"And great mining profits that could be made from exploiting them," Khaajd agreed. "This I do not doubt, my lord. What I doubt is whether those resources are <u>humankind's</u> to exploit."

"Yet if we did not exploit them," the duke asked, "would you?"

"No. The mountains would provide us with <u>different</u> resources. With goats to fill dragon bellies. With clean, mountain water to slake dragon thirsts. With caves in which to live. With a <u>home for our young</u>. Are those not resources of worth, my lord?"

"Yes," the duke murmured. "They are."

"And yet for the past two hundred or more years your people have systematically stolen our home from us." Khaajd's voice was soft. "I am far from old by the reckoning of our people, yet I once flew where Yullat now stands. I drank from the mountain stream that you dammed to form the lake above, the lake that destroyed you. I hunted for goats where <u>we now stand</u>. Now the goats are gone and the dragons are gone. None can live within fifty leagues of this place. Look around you, my lord. Look what your people have done to us. Tell me, are you surprised that dragons hate you?"

The duke sighed. "No, Khaajd. I'm not surprised. Were I a dragon I, too, might hate. Yet what of the other matter, the ..." he considered the number "... three quarter million humans who have lived in the mountains all their lives? As you said, a friend does not steal her friend's home. Would you, or your queen, steal <u>theirs</u>?"

Khaajd considered his words. "No. We do not want your people to suffer, neither I nor my queen. We want to be the <u>true</u> friends of the human race. The argument I apply to you I apply equally to us. A friend does not steal a friend's home <u>whichever</u> way round."

"Then it sounds to me as if you are proposing a freezing of the present," the duke said. "What is now will remain, but must not be added to."

"Not quite," Khaajd corrected. "There are four great cities in the mountains. These cities are so obviously a place of humans that they could no longer be anything else. Let then remain so with the blessing of Thaakumek and her people, but let them expand no further than their current city walls. Beyond your four city walls, however, are the mountains. Those are ours. They have always been and <u>must</u> always be. Yet within those mountains are many smaller human settlements, villages and towns that humans call home. Within those mountains are also mines, and through them wind roads. Let them remain there. No human will be forced to leave, no mine will be forced to close, no road will be broken, but there will be no more unless the dragon queen <u>herself</u> agrees to their construction. What is already there will become an outpost of humanity in <u>dragon lands</u>. Humans may live in those towns and villages, or work in those mines, but their liege lady will be Thaakumek and their laws will be those Thaakumek sees fit to impose."

The duke's jaw dropped in astonishment. "You're suggesting humans should be <u>ruled</u> by the dragon queen?"

"I'm suggesting those humans should be ruled by whoever is the <u>rightful ruler</u> of the land in which they live," Khaajd replied, "and that rightful ruler is the queen of dragons. The humans of the mountains should not fear Thaakumek's rule. She is noble and just, and will be so to all her people. Whoever or whatever they may happen to be."

"That would be a difficult idea to sell." The duke's voice still told of shock.

"Yet what better gesture could there be?" Khaajd asked. "What greater sign of genuine trust and goodwill between Thaakumek and yourself? We save the people of Yullat because you are genuinely our friends. You return the mountains to us because they are genuinely ours. Those who raise their voices against Thaakumek would have to do so knowing her wisdom had won our people the one thing they desperately need, their <u>home</u>."

The duke took a deep breath and released it very slowly. "How did you put it?" he asked. "Placing my neck in the jaws of fate?"

"Those were my words."

"I will need to give this some <u>very</u> serious thought," the duke said.

"I would expect no less of a wise ruler," Khaajd replied. "And, if truth be told, I have not yet suggested this idea to Thaakumek. She might prove as surprised as you were."

"Does Thaakumek know enough of human ways to be <u>able</u> to properly rule human people?" the duke asked.

Khaajd tongue wrapped. "No. Yet doubtless she will learn. Until she does she would greatly benefit from the assistance of a skilled and trusted human governor. Someone well known to the mountain humans, a face they will recognise and a voice that will reassure them. Perhaps you could loan her such a man."

The duke nodded. "Yes. That I could arrange." He frowned, thinking. "I need to speak to Thaakumek herself."

"Of course," Khaajd said. "This I shall arrange."

# Chapter Seventeen

A group of men, women and children gathered in the bright cold of a mountain, winter afternoon. Twenty-two villagers, their faces filled with doubts. Their voices reduced to murmurs.

Facing this group were three men and, behind them, three vast shapes. Well, two vast and the third dwarfing even those two.

"Men and women of the village of Han Ballas." It was the duke. "I am here to speak to you today of an agreement between the humans and the dragons. An agreement for peace, and for the good of both peoples. You will doubtless have heard many rumours and have many concerns about how this agreement might affect you and your village. I hope to be able to allay any fears you may have, and tell you of the safeguards that form a fundamental part of the agreement. Safeguards that exist to ensure you, the people of Han Ballas, suffer no ill as a result of the new understanding between the dragon and human peoples. Here to assist me in explaining this agreement are five good friends, both of mine and of humankind's in general. I present ..." he gestured as he gave the names "... Lord Norras Farron, Mr Aldon Torm, Thaakumek queen of dragons, Khaajd and Bhuul, the queen's battle master. We are all here to answer your questions, any and all questions you may have, and I personally guarantee they will be answered honestly and in full ..."

"Then let's begin with one," an angry voice cut in. "Is it true we have been sold out to the dragons? Yes or no, my lord? One word!"

The duke looked towards the man who had spoken. "I am permitted only one word? Very well, that word is 'no'. You have not been 'sold out' to anyone. Now, if you will permit me a few more words so that I can tell you the full truth rather than just part of it, I shall tell you what actually has happened."

He paused, looking at the gathered people. There were suspicious scowls, but accompanied by silence.

"The dragons are a mountain people," he continued, "and for thousands of years these mountains have been their home. In more recent years we humans have moved into their mountains, building villages such as yours and sinking mines. We have done this without the agreement of the dragons, and this has caused great resentment and enmity between the two peoples. Violent death, fear and great suffering have been the price paid by human and dragon alike, yet with this agreement our differences are resolved. With this agreement Thaakumek herself fully and absolutely accepts that your village is your home, that your houses are yours to live in, that your mine is yours to work and that you should be able to live in peace, goodwill, safety and prosperity here. What have you lost with this agreement? You have lost the fear of dragon attack. You have lost the risk of sudden death or destruction of your village. Honestly, ladies and gentlemen, are these things you would rather keep? What have you gained with this agreement? You have gained a powerful and noble friend in Thaakumek. A friend who is on your side. Is that not worth the gaining?"

"How can we trust this ..." the voice echoed with doubt "... dragon queen?"

"Let us ask her directly!" the duke suggested and turned to where Thaakumek stood behind him. "How can these people trust you, queen of dragons?"

Thaakumek's head shifted slightly as she looked at the gathered villagers. She addressed them directly. "I cannot ask for your trust," she murmured. "I cannot demand it. I cannot even expect it. There is one thing and one thing only that I have the power to do. I can be <u>worthy</u> of your trust, and so I shall be whether you can find it in your hearts to trust me or not. I shall act with justice, honour, fairness and decency towards this village and all the villages of the mountains. Not just today and tomorrow. Not just this week and next. This year, and next year, and <u>every year I remain alive</u>. This is my absolute promise to you and to all other humans who live in dragon mountains. Of course I hope, once you have seen my words become my actions, that you will come to have faith in both. That is something only you can do, and only you can decide, yet whatever you do I will not fail you. Even if you cannot trust me I will <u>still</u> not fail you. My <u>own</u> decision has already been made, and I am committed to it with my whole heart."

"So you're telling us there will never be another dragon attack?"

"I wish I could," Thaakumek replied, "yet I cannot give that guarantee. That may not sound reassuring, but it is <u>honest</u>. Just as there are human bandits who attack the innocent while they travel the roads, there are also dragons who do not abide by the rule of <u>my</u> law and <u>my</u> command. Criminals and villains are not purely human phenomena. Yet just as your duke strives to protect the innocent and law abiding from the criminal, so will I. If a dragon attacks an innocent human then that dragon will be declared a criminal and will <u>face my wrath</u>. I will not have <u>my people</u> abused without expending every effort I can to right that wrong, and with this agreement you <u>are</u> my people as much as any dragon that lives."

"I would add one thing, if I may," the duke said. "I offer a guarantee to all humans who will come under dragon rule with this agreement. If you find it impossible to accept the new arrangements then your home, your workshop and any other properties you have here will be bought from you for a <u>good and just price</u> so that you can move freely to somewhere else without suffering unfair loss. This guarantee will remain in place for a <u>full year</u> from the first day that your village comes under dragon rule. I sincerely believe that if you accept this offer, sell your homes and move out you will come to regret that decision, but the offer is there for those who genuinely cannot accept Thaakumek as their liege lady."

There was a murmur among the crowd. A voice questioned. "If we want to leave we can? You will give us a fair price for our homes and properties, my lord?"

"I will."

"Then," the man said, "I suspect the dragon queen will find herself ruling empty villages and silent mines!"

"I doubt it." It was a new voice to the debate. Khaajd. "You think your mine would remain silent when gold was to be made from working it? Good and safe gold, as will be seen by all when my queen honours the promises she has made to the people of the mountains? No indeed! The duke may be forced to buy some homes, workshops and mines, but I assure you he will sell them well once people realise how good, and profitable, peace can be. You have the chance to be there at the beginning of a new era in the mountains. You also have the option of not being. Choose wisely, people of Han Ballas, because you only get to choose once."

A murmur rose from the crowd. Heads turned and whispers were exchanged. Hands gesticulated. Heads nodded and shook. Torm leant close to the duke's ear and whispered. "I think that might have done it, my lord. Well done Khaajd! No-one likes the idea of someone else enjoying the good fortune that fate says is rightfully theirs."

\*

Three months later Khaajd found herself, once more, standing by the pool outside her cave, gazing at her reflection in the water. Just as she had been that time before, she was brought back to the present by the sound of her queen's voice. "Do the dead still haunt you, my friend?"

Khaajd looked up, meeting Thaakumek's green eyes with her own. "Yes," she admitted, "and I believe they always will, but perhaps they are beginning to forgive me."

"Or you are beginning to forgive yourself." Thaakumek offered an alternative.

"Maybe," Khaajd murmered. Then she considered a moment. "So what of the world beyond my pool and my reflection?"

The queen tongue wrapped. "Of that there is much to say. I may have never stopped being the queen of dragons but now, for the first time in many years, I truly believe myself to be the queen of the mountains. There is still mistrust of my rule among the mountain humans, and I suspect there will be for many months or years, but the initial rush of people wanting to take the duke's gold and leave has stopped. Those that remain might not be as confident as I would like, but they are confident enough to wait and see what happens. As long as I remain true to the promises I made them, their confidence should remain or even grow."

"You will remain true," Khaajd murmured. "Of that there is no doubt in my mind."

"Yes," Thaakumek murmured, "I shall. Farron is a great help. He acts as my governor of humankind, and he throws himself into that role with great energy and effort. In truth all I have to do is ensure dragons leave humans in peace, and Farron does the rest. Never has ruling a people seemed so easy. I fear I might slide into sloth and idleness!"

Khaajd tongue wrapped. "A little idleness would do you no harm," she observed. "You have had enough worry of late. Yet what of your opponents among dragonkind?"

"They still oppose," Thaakumek said, "and their voices are sometimes still objectionable to the ear, yet they are not as loud as they were. The human duke made a great show of halting all work on the two new cities his people were building, and then an even greater one of dismantling them. The sight of those not-quite cities vanishing before dragon eyes worked wonders in the hearts of unsure dragons. They saw a real change. A real difference. Many who were dubious now feel certain enough to argue against my opponents, and the opponents themselves have grown far less absolute in their beliefs."

"Good. And Yullat?"

"The duke has just declared Yullat is no longer a city of disaster," Thaakumek said. "The emergency is officially over, even though there remains a great deal of rebuilding to do. We are now reducing our flights into the city as Yullat becomes better able to support itself."

Khaajd raised her head and allowed herself a slight flash of celebratory flame. "That is excellent news!"

"There is more," Thaakumek added. "The duke has declared that the priorities for rebuilding are homes, shops, workshops, places of worship, administrative buildings and schools. He has stated that the defences against dragon attack are the lowest of all priorities and that, in truth, they will probably never be rebuilt at all. Yullat is to become a statement in brick and stone of the peace between our two peoples."

"There will be those who oppose that decision."

"Indeed there are," Thaakumek confirmed. "The duke has some very vocal opponents among his own people. Yet he also has many supporters. People who see, as he does, the good that is happening. There have been a few incidents where a damn fool dragon has done something destructive and stupid, but when I see such insanity I act to right the wrong as best I can. The fool is dealt with, usually by Bhuul and usually not in a manner of his liking. The humans see that I take action and approve of what they see."

"That's all a good queen can do."

"So what of <u>you</u>, Khaajd?" Thaakumek's head tilted a fraction as she looked and assessed. "I think you have put on some weight. Admittedly you are far from what you should be, but better surely?"

"I now believe the future is a place I want to be part of," Khaajd replied, "and that would be difficult if I starved myself to death."

Thaakumek looked long at her. "I shall go and get you some goats," she declared.

"No. You have done that enough of late. Now it's my turn. This time I shall hunt for my queen."

"Are you strong enough?"

"The goats may believe not." Khaajd tongue wrapped. "Unfortunately for them, they will be proven wrong!"

Thaakumek watched as Khaajd climbed high onto the ridge above, spread her massive wings, and launched herself into the air. The wing beats were powerful, strong and sure as Khaajd shrunk to a tiny speck in the sky. "Thank you, my friend," Thaakumek murmured to the vanishing dragon. "Not just for me and for dragonkind, but for everyone." She tongue wrapped. "Well, perhaps not for the goats. I wouldn't want to be one of them this day!"

Lightning Source UK Ltd.
Milton Keynes UK
UKOW02f2333110115

244303UK00002B/132/P